Praise for An

Cat & Th

"Quiet, chilling and absolutely thr........ .... Engver, *author of*
Winter Light

"A very unusual and powerful heart-wrenching read."
- D.L. Finn, author of In the Tree's Shadow

The Clock in My Mother's House

"Haunting, poignant, playful. Each one is a gem."
- Anne Goodwin, author of Matilda Windsor is Coming Home

"A haunting and wistful collection of short stories that will possess the
reader's imagination long after the last page has been turned."
- J.S. Watts, author of the Witchlight series

Small Forgotten Moments

"A spellbinding, intoxicating journey into the dark heart of obsession.
... another beautiful, heart-wrenching, epic masterpiece. I loved it."
Tom Gillespie, author of The Strange Book of Jacob Boyce

"A soulful tale of painting, secrets and longing, which draws the reader
into a world of mystery and memory - an enchanting read."
Leonora Meriel, author of The Unity Game

"It's beguiling, haunting, beautifully paced and it kept me hooked to
the very end."
Michael Walters, author of The Complex

THE BOATMAN

Also by Annalisa Crawford

ANNALISA CRAWFORD

THE BOATMAN

Lynher Books

ISBN: 978-1-7391608-5-2

THE BOATMAN
PREVIOUSLY PUBLISHED AS OUR BEAUTIFUL CHILD

First published by Vagabondage Press 2014
Revised edition by Lynher Books 2023

Cover by: Getcovers

To the real Boatman pub
and the ghost stories
we told each other

CONTENTS

THE TRAVELLER

ONE

The air is stagnant and thick. After days of sultry, persistent heat, a deep weariness is enveloping the town.

Music pours in from the beer garden—or rather, the paved area between the Boatman and the river which has slowly been assimilated into the pub's territory one table at a time. Most people are sitting out there, listening to the acoustic band. Some are tapping their feet to the soft melody in the air; others sing along.

It's cooler inside; it's always cold in the Boatman. With its low ceilings and thick stone walls, it should surely be warmer, cosier, somewhere to curl up and forget the stresses of the day.

"Must be the ghosts," said the barman with a wink, the first time I came here. I laughed, but even now, I still cast a glance around before choosing my seat.

The room is alight with a candle on each table; flames blink as people pass on the way to the bar. Shadows of lovers and friends magnified on the walls make the room crowded and muddled. Sometimes I count the shadows to make sure.

The table in the far corner is my favourite. Perfect for observing, perfect for making myself small and irrelevant, which is my aim. I set my sea breeze cocktail on the table and pull a book from my bag. It's a prop, a distraction, a way to divert unwanted attention.

I watch the stranger enter. As do the other three women in the room. We try to be subtle, sneaking a glance over our drinks or—in my case—my trusty book. We look up in clumsy unison, so he must have noticed, but he walks solidly towards the bar and faces the wall, pretending otherwise.

The stranger. Odd to think of him like that, specifically, when all the people in this pub are strangers to me. He's different; he doesn't belong either. At the bar, he drops a rucksack to the floor and catches the eye of the barmaid. She smiles widely, as I would. As we all would. After a brief chat, she gives him a key and puts his bag behind the bar.

Disappointed he's obviously taken, I can't bring myself to look away from his broad shoulders and blond hair which curls at the nape of his neck, or the muscular definition of his arms. He leans forward while he talks to her, and she laughs, handing over the pint she's been pouring and taking his money.

Female eyes avert their gaze conspicuously as he finds a table and drops into the chair. He closes his eyes and tilts his head to take the first sip, savouring the taste as though it's his very first. I almost feel the condensation clinging to the rim, the fine tingle of froth on my lips, the ice-cold lager sliding down my throat.

Women stare, caught up in fantasy, but as he scans the room, they dip their heads and shrink back into their chairs in an inverted Mexican wave.

I consider the rucksack, which was large and straining. So, not a stranger after all, but a traveller. That's a shame. Strangers tend to hang around; travellers leave.

I turn back to my book, a slim volume of poetry by an unknown poet, given to me as a just-because present by an ex-boyfriend—or so I thought at the time. On the inside cover, he'd scrawled, *I will always remember you.* My heart jumped when I read it. He accepted my thanks and my kisses, and I thought myself in love. Ten days later, he ran away to Derbyshire with an exotic dancer named Topaz. Suddenly, his awkward phrasing made much more sense.

I don't read it. I turn the pages occasionally as though I am.

When I look up to reach for my drink, the Traveller is resting his head in his hands, his elbows leaning on the table. His eyes are closed, and there's a furrow between his brows. He looks desolate, achingly intense. His girlfriend behind the bar has barely noticed, but I'm intrigued. I imagine the power of his arms sweeping me into an embrace; my stomach flutters nervously. He opens his eyes, brushes his hands through his hair, and catches me staring. He smiles, and I fluster, blushing absurdly. The next moment, he's standing in front of me, casting a shadow across the table.

"Mind if I join you?" The words are precise, smooth, as though he's used to approaching women in bars but not overly fussed if they decline. His voice is deep; he is enchantingly enigmatic.

"Won't Rona mind?"

"Who?"

"Your girlfriend. At the bar."

He looks back at the bar in confusion. "Um…"

"She gave you a key."

"Right, yes. I'm staying here for a few days. They have rooms upstairs."

With unanticipated delight, I remove my bag from the adjacent seat and smile.

He reaches for my book as he sits. "Joel Bunton. I didn't think anyone else had heard of him."

"It was a present."

"Oh. Do you like it?"

"It's okay…" I look into his slate grey eyes, framed by long black lashes, and momentarily forget what I was going to say. "This isn't *yours*, is it? You're not Joel Bunton?"

"Ah, no."

"He has a clever way of seeing things, I guess, but." In fact, the words make no sense—they squirm around on the page, trying to be intelligent and erudite, yet failing.

"Yes. But. I completely agree."

He flicks through the pages, settling on something that catches his interest, then hands it back with a self-conscious grin. "Of all the things I thought we'd be talking about when I came over, Joel Bunton wasn't one of them." His eyes soften, and his lips part seductively as he takes a sip of his pint. "I'll start again. Hello, I'm Murray."

"Quinn."

"It's very nice to meet you, Quinn. That's an unusual name." He spends a minute or so coming up with names it could be short for. Quinnibet becomes his favourite. "You're waiting for someone?"

"No. Oh…" I realise I've been glancing at my watch. "Not tonight."

"Good."

"So, you're travelling?"

When he looks puzzled, I remind him of his rucksack.

"Not really. Kinda. I don't know."

"That covers all the options."

He laughs. "It all depends," he says with a potent pause. "It's lonely by myself, sometimes."

I pretend not to hear and sip my drink. When I finish, he buys me another, and I buy the round after that. It's almost dark. The band is packing up, people are drifting home. I hadn't realised it was so late, but I choose not to mention it.

A breeze rushes past us and the candle in the centre of the table jumps. From somewhere beyond the horizon, a tremble of thunder creeps through the dark sky. The few people left outside shriek and scramble indoors as rain splinters onto the hot pavement.

"I love rain," I say, as we both turn to the window. Lightning shatters the sky.

"Come on, then. Let's walk."

"In this?"

"Why not?"

It's cooler outside now. The oppressive air has been diluted. We're drenched from the moment we step onto the pavement. My dress clings unflatteringly to my hips and stomach, and my

Tanya hesitates. I'm defiant. She doesn't have the authority, as much as she would love it. She holds my gaze for a moment. "Get to work. And get yourself some mints."

I brush past her. She allows me as far as the door.

"Oh, and the ladies' needs unblocking."

TWO

I like the stagnant silence of this my flat when I get home. Turning the key and immediately feeling relaxed, knowing what to expect on the other side of the door. When I realised how much of my wages I'd have to spend on rent, I considered looking for a flat-share instead. But I'm glad I didn't. I love the feeling of not having to converse, of not sharing my space, of not being on show all the time. I spent three weeks, between leaving Leeds and coming here, sleeping on a friend's sofa, and it did not go well.

Depending on how tiring work has been, I sometimes fall back into bed, throwing my clothes onto the floor and curling up beneath the duvet. Today, however, I'm surprisingly awake. I make toast and scrambled egg, plunging my finger into the bread to test for freshness and holding the milk briefly to my nose. I switch the TV on to a repeat of *Death in Paradise*, legs stretched out, enjoying the sensation of sitting for the first time in hours and doing nothing.

The credits roll; the murder is solved for another day. I flick to the news channel.

"And the headlines this afternoon... A body has been found in a flat in the centre of Leeds. Police are appealing for witnesses... The MP at the centre of..."

I stare in disbelief. I turn the TV off, then back on again. The newsreader has returned to the top story. The screen shows the

THREE

I'm at the Boatman again. The flat was closing in on me; the ghosts of my past were threatening to creep out. I was compelled by the news, by the same words repeated over and over—I couldn't bear it a second longer. When I stepped into the street, I felt as if I'd been expelled from a dark prison and thrust into a shining spotlight. So, I fled to the pub—the sanctuary, I imagine, of so many fugitives and renegades across the centuries. If ghosts did exist, I'm sure they would exist here.

Murray is perched on a stool at the bar, talking animatedly to a woman beside him when I arrive. I expected him to be here—*wanted* him to be, even. I need to banish those thoughts.

I watch through the window, pretending I'm *not* watching. When I feel self-conscious, I glance towards the river, convincing myself I'm enjoying the view before entering the pub. My eyes are drawn back. Whatever he's saying is obviously amusing. His companion grins and touches his arm, lingering on his perfect biceps. But when he offers her another drink, she shakes her head and points to the door. He holds her hand, and she laces her fingers with his before unfurling them one at a time and kissing his cheek.

I walk in as the woman leaves, and Murray's eyes dart from her to me. How easy it seems for him to switch his attention. "Ah, the delightful Quinnibet!"

"Quinn's fine."

"I thought for a moment I'd be stuck talking with Niall here." He nods his head towards the barman.

"Don't let me stop you."

"Can I buy you a drink?"

"Was that your girlfriend who just left?"

He instinctively glances towards the door. "Is everyone in your life cosied-up and paired-off? Can't a man simply have a pleasant conversation with someone?"

"So, she leaves, and you move straight on to the next target? Nice."

"Uh." He slaps a hand against his heart. "I'm wounded you should think so little of me."

"I don't think anything of you." I wince at my severity and try again. "I don't know you well enough."

"Ah." He finishes his pint to hide the smile.

There are a couple of tables between us. I'm aware of several people observing our exchange. Flirting with an audience is new to me. Flirting? Am I? Is *he*? It's been a while since I let myself have a bit of fun.

"Well," Murray says, "I'm having another. What d'you fancy?"

The woman on a table behind me chuckles. "Him, right?" she whispers, and I blush.

Decision time: yes, or no? I can convince myself all I like that I'm here for the friendliness of the pub and the relaxed aura, but if I didn't want to see Murray again, surely I could have found somewhere else to go tonight.

"Lager. Thank you."

The woman at the table behind me isn't wrong. Am I being obvious or is it the consensus among all women? It seemed to be last night, when we were all taken aback by the stranger who walked through the door, but without the rain and thunder and tension it brought, this evening is more casual, more ordinary. Perhaps I was the only one to fall under the spell.

Murray takes our two pints to a table, and I follow. "This used to be my local," he says, sipping the drink while standing to peruse some of the old pictures on the wall. He's lost for a moment in the photos, reaching out to one of them but stopping short of touching it.

"I thought you were new to the area."

He sits. It's a small table; we're suddenly very close. "I grew up here. Moved away a few years ago. Thought I'd pop back and look up some old friends, see what's happening these days, that kind of thing."

"How's it going?"

"Good. New friends are better, though."

I smile.

"What about you? Are *you* local? I'm sure I'd have remembered you if you were."

"No. I came here a couple of months ago."

"Where from?"

"London," I say slowly.

"What brought you to this tiny town?"

"Fancied a change. Put a pin in a map."

We sit in silence for a while, awkward and uncertain. Murray looks around the room, his eyes lingering on two women who've walked in. He turns back reluctantly.

"You don't have to sit with me, you know. I'm happy on my own. I've got my book." I hold it aloft. I fished it out of my bag when he was distracted.

"You can't *still* be reading it. No one finds poetry that engrossing. Especially not *this* guy."

"Why not *this* guy?"

He snorts derisively. "He *may* have been on my uni course. He *may* have got this thing published in his second year and gloated about it for the entirety of the third."

"Not that you're bitter…"

He chuckles. "No, of course not."

Another pause in the flow. Another gaping hole. "I meant it. You don't have to sit here with me. I don't want to cramp your style."

"You're trying to get rid of me!"

Am I? Maybe. It's dangerous, isn't it? Two strangers in town. If anything happened, no one would know or care.

My drink is almost finished. "Actually, I need to make a move."

"Do you have to? It's early. We could..." He struggles with what we could do. The more he thinks about it, the more he seems to give up on the idea.

"Yes, I really do." I bend to retrieve my bag from the floor and —inexplicably—kiss his cheek on my way back up, enjoying the look of disorientation on his face. I dance around the tables towards the door without looking back.

I pass two pubs on the way home, both enticing me inside with live music from one and general mayhem from the other. A couple of men having a half-hearted tussle bump into me as I pass; both stop and bow deeply.

I like this town. It's a shame I'm not planning to stay.

Why aren't I? Because I never do, even when I meet nice people and feel settled. In fact, that's when I'm most *likely* to leave. They called Steve a loner on the news, but actually, it's me. I like sitting in pubs and cafes alone. I like wandering the streets and listening to conversations I'm not a part of. I like pleasing myself.

I pass the memorial garden—a small plot between a church and a car park to commemorate the two world wars—and shiver. Sometimes, if I close my eyes and listen, I hear voices. So many voices. Not ghosts, but echoes of the past, the saturating history of an ancient settlement. Not ghosts, but movement in the corner of my eye when I know I'm alone; footsteps behind me; the tingle of skin as if someone has rushed past me.

Not ghosts. *Ghosts aren't real.*

Another couple of minutes, quickening my pace, and I'm home. I throw my bag onto the sofa and stand in the long hall between the main room and my bedroom. I can't get Murray out of my head, though it's best for both of us if I do. It wasn't the plan—to come here, meet someone, stay. It's never my plan.

I make coffee, realising as I'm pouring the milk it's a silly idea, that I should root out the camomile tea left behind by a previous tenant, and more suited to the late hour. I drink the coffee anyway and resign myself to another sleepless night.

The walk to work clears my head, sauntering through the streets in the languid hours. I try to speed up, try to care enough about keeping the job so I'll make an effort. But I can't because I don't.

Our early customers are people who work on the industrial estates surrounding us—the delivery drivers and mechanics and the guys from the recycling centre. They're either just starting their day or just finishing it. They order large break-fasts and sit alone in opposite corners of the room, fixed on their phones, trying to block out the tedium. Same as me. Same as us all.

I idly wipe the tables, fill the sugar bowls with little sachets, and hunt down ketchup bottles that have been misplaced again.

Jen stands beside me. "The guy at the counter wants you to serve him."

"Piss off, I'm busy. Do it yourself."

"Trust me, I tried. He's gorgeous. But, sadly, he asked for you." She smirks.

Murray is leaning against the counter, staring at the menu. "Hey, fancy seeing you here. Can I have a regular coffee please, and"—glancing at the menu again—"a breakfast bap?"

"What are you doing here?" I tug at the tabard of this wretched uncomfortable uniform, avoiding eye-contact.

"I'm... hungry?"

"How did you know I'd be here?"

"I didn't." He smirks. "What, you think I followed you? You think I'm stalking you?"

"Of course not," I say slowly. Followed me? Did he? Would he? *Don't be stupid*, I tell myself, yet, I find myself backing away. "But we're all the way out here, while you're staying on the other side of town. There are nicer places on the high street, you know."

"What can I say? Things to do, people to see."

"How was the rest of your night?"

"Well, it's eight-thirty. I'm up, I'm here, and I'm sober." He shrugs. "I went home. No one worth talking to after you left." He glances sideways to where Jen is trying to edge herself into his awareness. He pretends to ignore her, but he's checking her out. Everyone does.

She's slightly taller than me, blonde, pretty—beautiful, I guess, if we didn't have to wear our hair scraped back out of the way. Her makeup is flawless, and her pout is contrived and obvious, unless you're a smitten bloke, I suppose. So, when Jen moves in and Murray glances sideways, I turn to make the coffee and grab his bap from the hatch. Let them have each other, I don't care.

I slap the items on the counter. "Cash or card?"

"What time do you finish?" he asks, counting out change from his pocket and handing me the correct amount.

"Two."

"Doing anything nice?"

"Sleeping, probably."

"Fancy a coffee? Not here, somewhere else. I'll pick you up."

Jen's serving the next customer. She wants to butt in, to interfere; she wants her share of the invitation. Maybe, if she wasn't there, I wouldn't say, "Sure, why not?"

"Great." He unwraps the bap and takes a bite. "See you then."

Murray isn't here at two. Jen hangs around for a few minutes, then snorts and asks why I thought someone like him would be interested in someone like me.

"He's not all that. He's pretty ordinary, really."

"Yeah, right. See you tomorrow." She's laughing as she walks to her car; laughing as she drives past and waves.

I wait until half-past, then go home. I should probably be annoyed. If it were anyone else, I would be. But I half-expected him not to show up—he seems the type to drift around and not give a damn about much at all.

Miffed, that's all I am. I'll go home, like I planned, eat toast and watch TV for a bit. I'll probably fall asleep on the sofa, and then this evening, I'll go out again. Maybe not to the Boatman, maybe somewhere different. Different is probably a good idea.

Steve is headline news again. I was hoping something would have superseded him by now—a government scandal, a teachers' strike, a new murder to snare public interest. I'm sickened every time I think of him lying there, all alone, waiting to be found. After so long, it might be impossible to uncover what happened. Tests may come back inconclusive. The police will gradually be drawn to other, more urgent cases. And that will be that. A life wiped out. A life that no longer matters.

There's nothing new to add to the story, but the media can't leave it alone. The newsreader flounders along on the same scant facts, trying to make them sound fresh and new, as though some progress is being made. One of his neighbours, who I don't recognise, tells the interviewer Steve was a lovely lad. Anything to get on the TV. *Watch the news tonight, Dorry,* she'll chatter on the phone later. *I'm on telly talking 'bout that lad that died.* I doubt she knew him at all.

I don't want to be reminded of Steve, of us, but I can't pull myself away—it seems disrespectful. He was indeed *a lovely lad*, a good person. I sigh, standing in front of the TV, plate in hand. I haven't even made it to the sofa yet, I've just been standing here. It's all so surreal.

"Okay," says Murray when I open the door. I haven't fallen asleep yet, but my eyes are heavy and my body is clumsy. "I'm sorry. I know I said I'd be there, and I wasn't, but I have a good excuse."

I stare blankly, muzzily. "What are you doing here? How the hell do you know where I live?"

"I asked at the diner."

"How the hell did they know?" I mutter and vow to confront whoever it was tomorrow.

"Do you want to hear it? My excuse—do you want to…?" His eyes dance beneath his fringe.

"No. I don't." I want to sleep. I want to stop Steve's image chasing me.

"Are you angry with me?"

"What? Why?"

His face widens into a relived smile. "Good." He pauses, moves forward a little as if I've invited him inside.

My eyes narrow. "For fuck's sake, Murray Don't you think of anything but yourself? The world doesn't revolve around you. You're one very tiny, insignificant piece of it." My face reddens, and my head throbs with exhaustion. "Do you think I want to see your stupid face everywhere I go? Do you think I *want* you to constantly hound me, to show up on my *doorstep*?" My voice is escalating.

He shrinks back, head bowed.

"Because I don't! I don't care if I never see you again!" I slam the door shut. He steps back quickly to avoid being hit. His outline remains in the frosted glass while I return to my flat and slam that door too.

I don't hear him leave, but when I look out of the bay window, he's not there. One lone lady is wheeling her shopping basket towards the high street. A seagull is pecking at a discarded pasty.

My eyes sting. I rub them with the back of my hand and realise I'm crying. I blink away the tears. I haven't cried for a long time. But now I've started, I can't stop. I lean against the wall beside the window and allow myself to go with it.

FOUR

Before going to Leeds, I was still at home with my parents and planning to settle down with Andrew, I guess. How foolish. We were children; we'd barely begun to grow up.

It was stormy the day I met him. All the important days in my life, so far, have been stormy. During summer storms—sizzling and humid—I meet men. During bleak, grey, swirling winter ones, I lose them.

We were on an activity week in Wales, volunteering with a youth group we were both attached to, although we hadn't noticed each other before. We were half-way up a mountain, appreciating the vast dramatic scenery. We'd been told this was a wonderful vantage point by the staff at the hostel, so we paused and waited for the others to catch up. It *was* stunning. You could see for miles and miles, uninterrupted; towns and landmarks looked like specks. So many variations of green and blue, of brown fields ripe for haymaking, and the tiniest sliver of sea. I took photos which, when I looked back later, were flat and lacklustre in comparison.

The aim was to reach the top by lunchtime and take the cable car back down after we'd eaten, but incoming rain was threatening to drive us back to the hostel early. Out across the Irish Sea, there was a flash of lightning.

"You look like you could use some coffee." Andrew was beside me when seconds earlier I'd been alone. All day we'd suffered the tiny cartons of apple juice supplied in the hostel's packed lunches.

"You've got coffee?"

"Sssh. Don't tell everyone, they'll all want some." He took a flask from his bag and poured out the steaming liquid. Caffeine flowed and I was energised again.

"Oh, this is heaven. Have you ever seen so much open space?" We were so small, so enveloped by nature.

"It's incredible, isn't it? It's the first time some of these kids have ever left the city."

My own upbringing wasn't much different. My parents worked hard for little money. Holidays were something my friends went on.

The trek leader made the decision to turn around once everyone had caught up with us, with much groaning from some of the stragglers who'd just arrived. We walked back together, Andrew and I, scooping up kids as they dawdled off the path, and tried to keep their spirits up. And when the rain came, we ran and laughed and got drenched.

"What are you doing this evening?" he asked, as we headed to our separate dorms. "Are you on chaperone duty?"

"No. Night off, thank God. Not sure I could handle another game of Charades."

"Fancy a pint at the pub?"

"Are we allowed?"

"It's our free time. I don't see why not."

That night, among the hectic hum of Welsh accents in the crowded village pub, we talked about all the unimportant things people talk about when they first meet and quickly moved onto our hopes and dreams, our plans. Andrew was on a gap year—volunteering with this group for a few months before heading to Morrocco for six months.

"Oh." My plans were non-existent. Certainly, I wasn't about to leave the country and do anything so worthy. I'd been having no luck finding a job, and I wasn't cut out for university. My life was depressingly mundane, and he seemed so exciting.

He leant across the table and kissed me. "I'm not leaving until after Christmas."

It was four months until Christmas. I smiled softly and ran my hand along his forearm. Anything could happen in four months.

And it did.

When the final day of the holiday arrived, Andrew asked for my address. Perhaps it was a mistake to give it to him. No, it *was* a mistake. We'd had a couple of drunken nights together—it was *never* a relationship.

But I got sucked in. I got involved when I shouldn't have. We messaged and video-called, spending hours talking nonsense, and I didn't know how to break up with him. I'd never ended a relationship before; I'd never been in one.

He met my parents. He travelled to spend the weekends with me. He bought my mother flowers each time he stayed. At Christmas, he said his plans had altered and he wasn't going to Morocco after all. He hinted we might look for a place together.

And I assumed I was in love.

My second mistake.

That's when he gave me the book of poetry. He'd found it in a second-hand bookshop and slipped bookmarks into the poems he said made him think of me. And he ran away with another woman—literally, ran. He was practically living with us by then. He packed his bag and left a pathetically feeble note. I always thought Andrew was different, that he was sincere and considerate and would always be there for me.

I cried when he left. I thought I would die of grief. But I was wrong. I live on.

***

The investigation into Steve Mayer's death is proceeding well, say the police. An informant has come forward with vital evidence. They also have a detailed description of the woman who'd been living with him before he died. And a photo fit.

Of course, I am the woman; and, of course, they want me to come forward as I might have vital evidence too. I am important. I discover this while sitting on a bus, reading someone else's newspaper. I thought it would be nice to get out and about on my day off, but now I'm conspicuous and exposed.

The owner of the newspaper is reading the sports news on the back page, and I'm staring at an uncanny likeness of myself on the front. I bury myself down into the seat, hunching my shoulders and imagining everyone must be seeing the same thing.

At the next stop, I squeeze through the people who have been forced to stand in the aisle and run to the nearest hairdresser. I crash through the door, halting abruptly as several pairs of eyes look up at me.

"Sorry," I whisper, and close the door softly behind me.

Two stylists are busy clipping and blow-drying, while another smiles and walks towards me, leaving some poor lady with her head partially tin-foiled.

"Do you have an appointment?"

"No, but I was hoping someone might be free?"

She tuts and runs her finger along the diary page. "Hang on." She walks across to the stylist with the clippers and returns to the desk. "Becky can fit you in after her lady. It'll be twenty minutes or so."

"Perfect. Thank you."

I flick through a couple of the magazines on the small coffee table beside my chair, head down, hiding away. I check my phone for messages, but there aren't any. I research train tickets, choosing destinations at random. It's time to move on. I've been in town too long. How many other people have seen that picture? I don't want to be involved; I want a simple life, in the shadows, hidden away.

Steve used to say I'd never settle down. A peculiar thing to say, perhaps, when we'd been living together for eight months. But he peered at the holdall in the corner of the bedroom, clothes not fully unpacked, and saw something I'd perhaps not seen myself.

To me, I was being lazy. Couldn't be bothered to hang clothes in the space he'd made for me or to fold them into a drawer. He was right, of course. Six months later and I was gone again. Nothing went wrong like it did with Andrew. Steve didn't cheat on me, we didn't argue. It fizzled out. What else is there to say?

Murray unexpectedly pops into my head—his penetrating eyes, his sexy smile, the way he runs his hand through his hair. There's something magnetic about him that I don't want to have to give up yet. The two of us could have fun together.

"Are you ready there?" Becky calls from the desk as *her lady* leaves. "What can I do for you today?" She's tying a cape around my neck and spritzing my hair with water.

"Something short. Chop it all off." On the shelf in front of me is a hairstyle magazine. On the cover, a woman with a cute pixie cut. "Like this?"

"Are you sure? You've got lovely hair, and this style is going out of fashion."

"Positive."

As my hair gets shorter, the shape of my face seems to change. My cheekbones become more prominent and my eyes sparkle. With the right makeup and maybe a change of colour, I wouldn't even recognise myself.

Perhaps I don't have to leave just yet. Perhaps I look different enough no one will think twice about me.

"Could you dye it?" I ask as Becky holds up a mirror to show off her handiwork.

"Of course. You'll need a patch test, but we could do it today, and I can fit you in for the colour at the end of the week."

I shake my head. "No, that's okay. This is fine."

On my way home, I pop into the pharmacy and pick up a box of dye. By teatime, I'm Fiery Red.

I don't go out tonight. The dying process was time-consuming and messy. I changed into my pyjamas, and I can't bear to get dressed again. I eat cereal for tea followed by ice cream and lager.

The dye has made my hair overly soft and I keep forgetting how short it is. I run my hands through it, slowly getting used to the feel of it. Several times, I go to the bathroom to check in the mirror. The more I stare, the more I'm enjoying not looking like myself.

The doorbell rings at half past eight, and I peek through the curtains to see who it is. I should have guessed. Murray's standing with a bottle of wine in his hands and a sheepish expression when he spots me looking at him.

"Can I come in?" he mouths.

I leave the window and open the door. "What do you want?"

"Wow, look at your hair. You look amazing."

"Thank you. But why are you here?"

"You weren't at the pub. I wanted to make sure you were all right."

"Do you often bring wine to a welfare check?"

"And... I wanted to apologise. I've been thinking about what you said. I didn't realise I was being so... so..." He frowns and shrugs. "I'm sorry." He holds out the bottle. "Here. If you don't want to let me in, you can at least accept this."

"A peace offering?"

"If you like."

I sigh. "I'm sorry too. It was bad timing. I was tired. It was a long day." I stand back and gesture towards my flat. "You can come in as long as you don't laugh at my pyjamas. I don't plan on changing into anything else."

His eyes scan over me, a smirk on his lips as he eases past me along the narrow corridor. "Fine by me."

I pour the wine. We sit together on the sofa, half-watching the end of a drama I've not been paying attention to. We sip the wine, and our hands accidentally touch. We talk about things of no consequence. I move a little closer, and then he does.

He looks as though he's going to say something profound. And then he kisses me.

*

40

I light the candles on the mantelpiece because I want it to be special. I want it to be one of those moments which is always with me. See a candle, think of tonight. See a flickering flame, remember Murray gazing down on me with those dark grey eyes; smell the soft floral fragrance, feel Murray's body sliding over mine.

He follows me closely, kissing the back of my neck as I light each one; his hands resting on my shoulders, combing through my newly-shortened hair. He kisses the back of my neck and turns me to face him. I shiver under his gaze, under his touch. His hands are warm as he eases my T-shirt up my torso and over my head.

He unbuttons his own shirt and slips it from his shoulders to reveal a firm, tanned chest. I nuzzle into the tufts of hair, kissing his shoulders and his neck, his jaw, his lips. He lowers me onto the sofa, manoeuvring to be on top. The warmth of his body radiates through me; I am engulfed by him.

The candlelight flickers as our bodies move in unison, making our shadows dance on the wall. I hold my breath, succumbing to the deep intensity of his gaze and his touch. And I am in love. Or I'm not in love, but right now, I can't tell the difference.

I wake to the sound of my bedroom door closing. I reach out to the warm space where Murray was lying. I stumble from my bed into the living room.

"I was trying not to disturb you," he whispers, pulling on his jeans.

"You're going."

"I have to." He looks sheepish. "I'm sorry, I wish I could—"

"No skin off my nose." I shrug, feign indifference. That's how one-night stands work, isn't it? No one cares.

He hops around to pull on one boot, then the other. I watch with my arms folded, as if I can't wait for him to be out of my way. It's the opposite of what I want, but I can't tell him, can I? He's leaving, which means he *wants* to leave.

He leans down and presses his forehead against mine. "God,

you're sexy. When can I see you again?" He repositions himself to kiss me, but I move slightly and he catches my temple.

"You know where to find me." I avoid his eye, unable to control my emotions. Cold and cutting is preferable to grabbing his arm and begging him to stay.

"You're cold. Go back to bed." He tries to kiss me once more, but this time I move backwards. He frowns, looks a little lost. "I'll see you soon, yeah?" He holds my gaze for a moment, then leaves.

I remain in the communal hall, my forehead pressing against the wall, wondering what the hell I'm doing. The sun shines through the glass of the front door. My upstairs neighbour wakes and begins to move around. The day begins and I am empty.

FIVE

Days pass. Several of them coming and going without really registering. At work, I gaze out to the main road and Tanya berates me for ignoring customers. I jump every time the door opens and find myself sighing when it's not Murray.

It's ridiculous, but I can't help it. I want to see him. Need to feel his arms around me and his lips pressing against my neck. But he's vanished. I haven't heard a word from him, haven't seen him at the Boatman, haven't caught sight of his sun-bleached hair disappearing walking ahead of me in the street.

He's moved on, I assume; possibly left town already. Or found his next conquest, and it'll be her bed he's extricating himself from, while I listen to my alarm clock piercing into the half-light. Somewhere out there, he'll be hastily dressing and sneaking away again.

The fact I know this means I should hate him. But I don't. I stare out of the living room window and imagine the lone footsteps echoing on the silent street are his.

"Stop this," I tell myself. I don't listen.

Tanya stands in front of me, clipboard in hand, tapping the list of tasks as she orders me this way and that. My head is swimming with Murray, with Steve, with what I left in Leeds; it's full of moving on, staying put, running away.

"You're not even listening," she says sternly.

I focus on the frown gathering between her eyes. "I did half of this stuff yesterday."

"And you did it badly."

I sigh and pinch the bridge of my nose. "I did it perfectly well, but you like to make my life a misery and this is all you have to attack me with."

"No, this is about having standards—something you're very much lacking."

"Oh, get stuffed."

Her eyes widen; her cheeks flush. "You're on your last warning, Quinn."

"Consider me warned." I pause, not quite sure what I'm going to do next, and then I turn on the spot and walk away. I'm in our small car park before I realise it. Striding down the road before I have chance to think.

"Oi. Quinn. Wait."

Jen runs after me. "Have you quit?"

"I'm not sure. Did she send you after me?"

"No." But she glances back along the road. I imagine Tanya's followed her, crouching behind a convenient bush to eavesdrop. "What will you do?"

"Dunno. Same as I always do, probably."

"What's that?"

"Go to the pub." I walk away, leaving Jen gawping.

The Boatman in the middle of the afternoon is a noiseless, eerie place. The heavy wooden door creaks as I open it. Chris, the landlord, is leaning on the bar, staring at his phone. An elderly couple sit with pints, holding hands but technically ignoring each other. One guy in a suit is reading a paper, another has a dog nestled at his feet, dropping crisps for it to snaffle. Lonely people gathered together to feel less alone.

And me.

Chris looks up. "Hi. What can I get you?"

Briefly, I think about leaving again, finding something else to do on this warm, sunny day. Outside, on the green, people are lying on blankets and eating picnics. They're watching the boats and the train going over the bridge. They have toddlers sleeping in buggies or playing on the little train-shaped climbing frame.

"I'll have a cider, please."

"Haven't seen you for a few days. Thought you were becoming a regular."

"Had a few things on." I consider asking if Murray's been in but bite my tongue to prevent myself.

I sit alone and think about the job I almost certainly don't have anymore and next month's rent I now won't be able to afford. I open the map app on my phone and idly move it around. Is it time for my pin yet?

A shadow falls across me. Murray? I immediately chastise myself for being so eager.

It's not. It's Jen. "I thought you could do with some company," she says, putting a glass of wine on the table.

"Actually, I'm good, thanks."

"I thought you'd like someone to talk to." She hangs her jacket across the back of the chair and sits.

"I was happy by myself."

"You don't have to talk, but I'm here now, so, cheers." She clicks her glass against mine, immune to the hostility I'm forcing in her direction.

"How did you know I'd be here?"

"You said you would."

"No. I said, *the* pub, not which one."

"Oh." She shrugs. "So, how's it going with that guy?"

"What guy?"

"The guy who ordered the breakfast bap and wouldn't let me serve him."

"Oh, him. It's not. I haven't seen him."

"That's a shame. He seemed nice."

"I guess."

"Does... he... come here often?" Her eyes scan the room as if expecting him to be lurking in the corner.

"Wouldn't know."

"You met him here, didn't you? I remember you telling me."

I don't answer. I take larger gulps of my cider and plan to get out of here as quickly as possible. This is the longest conversation I've ever had with Jen and I'm not keen on it.

My pint is almost finished when Jen glances at the door and beams. "Look who's arrived."

"Funny." I slam the glass onto the table and stand to leave.

"No, honestly. Look."

I turn and meet his eye. Shit.

I came here because I wanted Murray to be here. But now he's here, I don't want him to be.

Murray blocks my path to the exit. I step left and he matches my move. I go right, he moves too. He's smiling, laughing.

"Can I get past?"

"You're not going already?"

I glare. "Like you care."

"You're not going to leave your friend all alone, are you?"

"I'm sure she'll find someone to talk to."

Jen smiles widely. "Let her go if she wants to. I'm Jen, and I'm hanging around for a bit."

Murray leans forward. "Stay," he whispers, his warm breath on my neck causing a shiver.

"Whatever."

Murray goes to the bar. Jen scowls at me. I turn the chair to face away from the table, looking out of the window. There's an old-fashioned rowing boat slowly making its way upriver. Despite the sun and warmth, there's a strong breeze, and the water is choppy, but it looks like the rower is barely having to put in any effort at all. Oh, to be out there today, free from everyone.

"Quinn's told me so much about you," Jen says when Murray returns. Two pints and another glass of wine. "It's nice to meet you properly."

"And what's she been telling you?" His elbow is on the table, his chin resting on his hand. Talking to Jen but looking at me.

"Nothing," I say, rolling my eyes.

"I couldn't possibly divulge," Jen says at the same time. "But I do hope it's all true."

"Nothing," I say again.

Murray smiles with a wink. "Well, I can assure you, it probably is."

I sigh. "Do you really need me here?"

"No," says Jen.

"Always," says Murray at the same time.

I was close to leaving, again, but the irritation on Jen's face at his reply makes me want to stay. He's smooth. I don't know what game he's playing, but I'm curious. I lean back in my seat, take my pint, and sip it slowly.

SIX

I wake at six with the frantic panic I've overslept and will be late again. Then I remember: I walked out, I quit. I have no job.

So, I lie back and doze and think back over the afternoon and evening with Murray and Jen. Jen who stayed the entire time. It was his own fault. I could have warned him. I could have found a way to engineer Jen and me leaving and him coming to mine later. But I didn't. I sat and drank and ignored his hints. I bought another round. I made sure Jen had a night she would definitely forget. If she's on shift this morning, I imagine she'll be late.

I wander into the kitchen to make coffee. I scan the fridge and cupboards for something to eat. I pour cereal into a bowl with just enough milk to make it damp—I've got to conserve my rations now. Milk is more important in coffee than it is in cereal.

In the living room, I slump on the sofa and turn on the TV. Morning television is a strange phenomenon. People renovate houses, and buy antiques against the clock, and rescue others from being scammed. On another channel, they repeat comedies first shown twenty years ago. On another again, it's British comedies from *forty* years ago. More channels than ever, but apparently much less interesting stuff to view. I avoid anything news-related.

There's a square shadow on the curtains I've only just noticed. I open them to find a note stuck to the window. It's from Murray. *Phone me*, it says, with his mobile number underneath.

The cheek! He could have asked for my number last night. He could have not flirted with Jen all evening in front of me if he was still interested. He could have helped me walk her home rather than leaving us on the corner with a cheery wave.

"Piss off."

Phone me, the note says as if I'll drop everything and go running to him.

Piss off! Yet I probably will. It's an opportunity I can't pass up —he's chasing me.

I eat my breakfast and sip my coffee and ease myself into the morning, and after an hour or so, I dial the number.

"What do you want?" On the TV, someone is fawning over a weird ornament of a child and a pony.

"Good morning, Quinn. How's your head?"

"Fine. What do you want?"

"You don't sound happy."

"If you don't want anything, I'm hanging up. I've got better things to do than talk to you all day."

"I was going to knock, but the curtains were closed. I thought you might have been asleep."

"Why?"

"Because I wanted to see you. Can we meet for a coffee?"

"Why?"

"I thought we could have a chat. Nothing serious."

Why does it always sound serious when someone says that? "When?"

"Whenever. Now?"

A dull headache is beginning to form; I press my fingers into my temples. Now. That's more serious than a simple chat. I bite my nail.

"Why don't you come here?" I grimace. No, I didn't mean that. Not here. Out. We'll go out.

"Okay," he says slowly. "I'll see you soon."

"Murray, wait..."

He's already hung up, and I don't phone back.

*

I open the windows to let fresh air inside; the flat is suddenly airless and stale. It's warm again. Summer isn't letting go easily.

I can't settle while I'm waiting for Murray. I get dressed, rinse my breakfast dishes, empty the bin, put the bag outside. I'm boiling the kettle when he rings the buzzer. I tap the counter. I could pretend I'm out. But if he has something to say, I need to hear it. He buzzes a second time. I bite my nail. On the third one, I open the door, and I'm nervous.

"I'll be leaving soon," he says once we're settled in the living room with our coffees.

I nod my acknowledgement, though I'm unsure why it's such a big announcement. He stares at the carpet, perched forward in the armchair opposite me. We're intriguingly shy and awkward with each other, despite our night together.

"Cake," I declare abruptly. "My hangover cure. Lemon drizzle —always works."

In the kitchen, I unbox the cake and lean against the worktop, taking deep breaths. I return with two plates, the cake, and a large knife which glints in the stream of sunlight.

"I want you to come with me."

I cut two large slices and pass a plate to Murray. He hesitates, then accepts it, holding it aloft as though he's not sure what to do next.

"Did you hear me?"

"Why? We barely know each other. Why not Jen, or the other woman I saw you with?"

"Because...."

"I don't see you for days and then you show up and flirt with someone else in front of me. Is that how you treat people you like?"

"I was beginning to think you didn't care." A smile fills his eyes and sparkle indulgently. A genuine smile.

"I *don't* care." But even as I say it, the thought of Murray not being here makes me unhappy. More so than the thought of Steve or Andrew did... does—and I'm unnerved by it. "Were you trying to make me jealous? Is that what this bullshit has been about?"

"No." He crosses the room and crouches in front of me so I have no choice but to look at him. And when I look up, he kisses me.

I thought I was in love with Andrew; I deceived myself, or I was deceived as a wild prank on the new volunteer. With Steve, I tried harder and never loved him while presenting a fitting impression to the contrary.

Murray confuses me. Quite simply, quite openly, I hate him. For the way he taunts me, keeps me guessing, plays endless games. And I love him. For almost the very same things. And for his exuberance and the vulnerability he tries to keep hidden; and for the way he's looking at me. I want him to hold me and never let go.

This complicates things, of course. It's not part of the plan—although there's never really a plan, is there? My thoughts judder to a halt. An unfamiliar sense of doubt spreads over me.

"Do you have to go?"

"I never stay in the same place for long."

"But this your hometown. Doesn't that make a difference?"

"It makes it worse."

"Suppose... I did... come with you." Murray is attentive. "What would we do?"

A slow, assured smile flows over him. He leans back, relaxes. "Anything we wanted."

"But." I shake my head. "It doesn't work like that."

"Why not?"

I pick up the knife, cut another slice of cake neither of us wants. I feel the weight of the knife and roll it against my palm.

"You remember the night we met? You asked me why I was sad." He moves to sit on the sofa beside me, half-turned to face me, waiting for my full attention. I put the knife back on the table. "I never told you the real reason."

My heart beats fiercely. I remain silent.

"That day was the anniversary of my best friend's death. Ten years ago. We'd been out drinking, and we got it into our heads we could *borrow* his neighbour's car. Just for the night. Put it back before this guy ever knew it was missing." His words are erratic, jumbled. His tone is clipped but calm, the voice of someone disturbed by their memories.

"I drove. We were going to swap over at some point, and he'd drive back. But we never got... I hit a tree, skidded along the road, straight into the central reservation." His hands are shaking, his eyes fixed on the floor. He laces his fingers together, trying to curtail the movement. "We bounced around before hitting a barrier on the opposite side. Dave was screaming. His legs were trapped. Blood all over him. I got off lightly, a few cuts. I knew I was in trouble. So, I ran away."

He stops. Swallows.

Silent for a long time. Ashen. Distraught.

"The first I heard he'd died was when Mum woke me up and told me. He'd died in the car before anyone came to help. She was crying, hugging me, saying over and over how glad she was I wouldn't be so stupid to do something like that, because look how tragically it can end." His eyes glaze over. In another moment, he blinks himself back into the room. "No one knows I was in the car."

"Why are you telling me this?" My voice is loud and harsh, and I realise Murray must have been whispering.

He stares at me, through me. The pause is tormenting.

"Because you know what it's like to run away, don't you? To have secrets?"

The chill runs the full length of my body. I stop. No thoughts, no heartbeat. Not a breath.

"I—I don't know what you mean."

He watches me for a moment. It seems longer. His eyes bore into me. When I can bear the tension no longer, I look away. I wrap my arms around my body and hunch forward.

Don't say it. Please don't.

Two kids walk past my window, kicking a ball to each other across the width of the street, a loud but indecipherable conversation flows between them. I look up. Murray doesn't. He holds his gaze on me as if wrestling with the thing he's going to say next.

Please don't say it.

"I... saw your picture in the paper. Your photofit." He scrapes his nails across his jeans.

"My picture?"

He nods. His pure grey eyes pin me to my seat.

"Oh." There's no point arguing.

"That's why you cut your hair, changed the colour. You're trying to hide."

He edges closer. I bow my head and feel hot, thick tears roll down my cheek. He rests a hand on my shoulder; his other hand pushes the kitchen knife slightly out of reach.

"You killed that man."

Murray thinks he can save me. He thinks killing Steve was a mistake, an accident. Poor Steve. Wrong place, wrong time; at least, it was for him. Sitting alone in the café, with Andrew's blood still staining my fingers and the decadent memory of his heart beating feebly against my hand, I was unsure what to do next, where to go, how to move on.

And then, there was Steve in front of me—the *right* place, the *right* time. A chance to recreate the perfect moment of life and death colliding, a profound almost impossible sensation. I held him, felt his spirit dance away.

If Murray thinks killing Steve was a mistake, what would he do if he knew about Andrew? That I'd tracked him and his dancer bitch to their lovely new house in Derby. That I'd lain in wait until he was on his own, walked in, cool and composed, and stabbed him? No time to reason or plead, no time to scurry away.

Would Murray care I'd waited on the corner afterwards, out of sight, for her to come home, to listen to her screams when she opened the door and found the carnage inside? Would it matter to Murray, sitting next to me, waiting for me to confirm or deny?

Revenge. Oh yes, it had been all about revenge right up until the moment when the knife plunged into Andrew's yielding flesh. Then it became more. Nature took over. Because it's natural, in the end, to want to be dominant, to win, to survive. Isn't it? I held the power in my hands. I held *him* in my hands. I looked down, not quite grasping what I'd done, with a sense of awe and fulfilment.

I smile as I recall it. Murray shifts uncomfortably. I look back at him.

"We could find somewhere quiet, remote. Live a simple life."

What is he doing? Why isn't he running? Am I not capable of this thing he's accusing me of?

I don't need to answer.

I've already snatched the knife and plunged it into his chest.

He doesn't realise for a moment. He looks at me with a tenderness I've never seen in anybody's eyes. Then he looks down at the blood and holds my hand against the knife. A *why?* touches his lips. His body weakens. His eyes close as he falls back into the sofa.

He opens his mouth, but no words, no sounds appear. Each breath rattles laboriously; I can hardly bear to listen. Murray has my hand in his, still extraordinarily strong and determined.

"Love..." he whispers. He closes his eyes and concentrates on forming the next word, his lips curling into the shape of it. And then he's gone. His face falls; his grasp abates.

Murray dies well. Not like Steve, with hate in his eyes. Not like Andrew, who flailed around, his blood spattering the walls.

Murray's blood is contained, marking a small section of the dusky pink upholstery.

I'll never get over seeing dead people—a perfection no one can take away from me. The half-smile on their face, the peacefulness.

Murray's fringe has fallen across his eyes. I half-expect him to brush it away. After a moment, I do it for him.

We stay there together; I'm in no hurry. I kneel beside him and hold his hand, already a little colder. I don't feel good. There was contentment to the way I felt with Andrew and Steve, an honesty to my actions and thoughts. But this... this is different. He loved me. He was trying to say he loved me.

Tension zig-zags my stomach. I want to vomit. I'm cold. I can't smile or feel joy. I can't do anything other than stare at Murray and tell him how sorry I am.

Eventually, sense prevails. I kiss Murray's forehead, slip my hand from his, and swallow down my regret. Life could have been good, travelling around, seeing the world through Murray's eyes. We might have settled down in a town like this one, had a baby, and a dog, and been happy. We could have been happy.

I stand and grab my holdall from the bedroom, already packed and waiting. I don't look back, can't look; it's too grotesque. I stop in the kitchen for a glass of water, and when I've finished, I place the glass under running water and let it fountain over the rim. I lock the door to the flat, then the door to the building, and post the key through the letterbox. I wonder, for a moment, how long Murray will lie there waiting to be discovered.

And then, as quickly as I arrived in this small, bewitching town, I vanish into the bright afternoon sunlight.

ELLA'S STORY

I am three, maybe four. It's dark. Very late or very early. The house is silent. I can't hear the comforting hum of the TV in the living room or Daddy tidying the kitchen, but I can hear the tick-tock clock in the hall, echoing in the shadows. I'm hugging my teddy bear, Alfie, and curled up beneath my duvet. Because there's a monster under my bed.

I'm holding my breath and being very quiet so the monster won't know I'm here. My eyes are shut very tightly—like when Mummy says, "Close your eyes, Ella, we've got a surprise for you," and it's a new guinea pig or a chocolate cake. I hear a whimper and I think it must be me because monsters don't get scared. Everyone knows that. A monster would roar loudly or growl like the tiger we saw at the zoo, and this sound, this little cry, is very soft, like a kitten when she's lost. I want Mummy.

I call out by accident, then hold my hands over my mouth and wait for the monster to crawl out. Almost straight away, Mummy and Daddy are standing over me. The light from the landing pours in and makes my bedroom look like it does in the daytime. All the shadows have vanished.

"Monster," I manage to whisper, before bursting into tears.

Mummy sits down on my bed and hugs me, folding her arms around me and smoothing my long blonde hair away from my face. I can smell the scent of fabric softener on her nighty, and the cream she uses on her face. She rocks me backwards and forwards, and I start to feel silly. How can a monster get into the house when Mummy and Daddy are here to look after me?

"No monsters, sweetheart," says Daddy, looking under my bed, and in my cupboard, and through my big pile of teddy bears in the corner.

"Just a bad dream," says Mummy, kissing my forehead. She lays me back down and strokes my cheek.

Bad dream? I remember now. It *was* a bad dream. But it wasn't about a monster.

***

I am twelve, maybe thirteen. The moon shines through the gap in my curtains, casting a shadow of Alfie, sitting on my ottoman, along the floor. I heard a noise. Or saw a figure darting along the edge of the room. Or something touched my cheek. I hold the duvet over my face, peering out from one corner, embarrassed because I'm twelve, or maybe thirteen, and far too old for such babyish fantasies.

We should go to the circus, said the girl—the woman—in my dream. It's what she always says, this woman I don't know, sitting in a circle of people. The others are shadows, but I know they're there. In the dream, they're my friends.

It fills out tonight; the narrative stretches and expands. I'm aware of the bracelet on my wrist, the orange shirt I'm wearing. And tonight, there's an ending. Oh, there's definitely an ending. I wake hot yet shivering, scared and uncertain, on the cusp of a scream. For a moment, I don't know where I am.

I felt a jolt from behind and I fell, from somewhere high. And I didn't stop falling.

If I close my eyes, I'll probably still be tumbling into the darkness. I'm dead, in the dream.

As I fell, I knew I was already dead.

*

When I open my eyes, it's morning. I should feel safe. I should realise it was just a nightmare. But it was so real, as though it has already happened.

I'm tired, like someone's pulling me down into the mattress, sucking my arms and legs into the tangle of springs. I can't move; I can't swing my legs over the side of the bed. I want to stay right here. I really don't want to go to school and sit in double maths in a hot, stuffy classroom.

"Time to get up, sleepy head." Mum walks in without knocking again, carrying a pile of washed and folded clothes. She dumps them on my chair, and tomorrow she'll tell me off for not putting them away. "We really need to buy you some new things. How about a shopping day at the weekend? We'll leave Dad at home and pop into town."

I hide under the blankets and stop listening.

She opens the curtains and pulls the duvet away from me. "Get up. Chloe'll be here in a minute."

When she leaves, I slide out of bed and shut the curtains again. I don't want to see Chloe. I don't want to see anyone. I'm going to die—that's what my dream is telling me. So what's the point of school or friends or anything?

"We're all going to die," Chloe says, as we stomp along the road to school. I didn't mean to tell her; it blurted out without warning.

"What if it's a premonition or something? What if I'm going to die *soon*?"

"Well," she says, kicking a can along the road and watching it roll back towards her. "Do you know the people in the dream?"

"No."

She shrugs. "So, it probably won't happen for ages then, if you don't even know who they are." She laughs. "And also, it's just a dream, weirdo."

Afterwards, I stop telling people stuff. If they're not going to believe me, why bother?

It's just a dream, I try to tell myself.

***

I am seventeen, maybe eighteen.

We should go to the circus, says the woman who has haunted my dreams for so many years. I sit bolt upright in bed, but the nightmare continues anyway. Once it's started it, doesn't stop until it's all played out, right up to the final, fatal end.

I haven't been to the circus in years. Not since school, says the man who sits on my left.

I'm working, says the second woman.

This is the first time these other people have spoken; their voices slice into the air. I've always known they were there, in the periphery, yet they've receded when I've turned to them. They're more defined, now, setting themselves firmly in my awareness.

The four of us have been sitting like this for years. I know the number of glasses on the table; I know what everyone's drinking. I'm familiar with the people on the tables nearby and the barman and the music which isn't a song I recognise. I know the stone-exposed walls and the low ceilings with black-painted beams. It never changes. It's a memory of the future, it seems.

We meet regularly, often straight from work. This I know.

I fall to my death. *This* I know too. No, not fall. Pushed. I am pushed. Hands shove me; I feel the malice and force. I wake gasping and flailing, desperate to cling to something to save my-self.

So real. Too real. *Just a dream*. Surely, it can't be anything else.

Given we're starting to turn eighteen, evenings with friends now revolve around the pub on the high street, with its large screen TVs showing the football and rugby, its loud music and weekend DJ sets, with its requirement for bouncers on the door.

"Uh, here again?" says Chloe when we're standing outside. The noise is already raucous, and the lights are flashing. She slumps against the lamppost.

"Best place in town!" everyone screams before diving through the door.

We remain outside.

"Do you wanna...?" She gestures towards the door, and I find myself saying no.

"How about going down to the river? The Boatman's supposed to be nice."

She sighs, looking at the open door behind us and then in the direction of the river. "Yeah, why not?"

It's not a long walk, although the steep hill down will make an interesting climb on our return.

"How's your revision going?" Chloe asks. She's the focused one. The girl who stays home on week days to study and is determined to reach her ambition of becoming a doctor.

"English, good. Philosophy, surprisingly okay. History, ah..." I exhale and shake my head. "It'll be a miracle if I get the points I need, to be honest."

"I wish I could help."

"Focus on your own stuff. My little creative writing degree is nothing to your medical one."

"You shouldn't put yourself down."

"Well, it's not like..."

"What?"

"Do you remember the dream I told you about, years ago, where I die? I still have it."

"Dreams are the brain's way of processing information. Things you're worried about, new things you've done or learnt during the day, that kind of thing."

"But it's been the same since I was little. It gets more vivid each time—more details are added in. It feels so real."

We reach the pub. Her hand is on the door when she says, "Forget about it. It's your mixed-up head doing strange things."

And then we walk into the Boatman for the first ever time, the pub from my dream.

***

I am twenty-three, maybe twenty-four. I roll over and search for Will's profile in the pre-dawn gloom. Although I'm an adult, although it's just a nightmare, I still gasp for breath when I wake, still hot and sticky. Still scared to go back to sleep.

Will stirs a little. Perhaps I could wake him so we can sit on our little balcony and watch the sunrise with mugs of coffee.

Ha! No! Will isn't that kind of man. He'd complain he has to go to work because he's got an important meeting first thing, and I've ruined his day by waking him up with some nonsense about the sunrise.

I used to think we were soulmates, Will and I. When we left uni and he was happy to follow me back to my hometown and found a good job in his field, I thought it was all so perfect. But it isn't. My soulmate would wake *me,* and we'd drag our duvet onto the balcony and curl up beneath it. Maybe we'd even start the night out there, falling asleep under the stars.

Here and now, in my bed, hot and sticky and scared, I'm three again, waiting for Daddy to tell me all the monsters are gone.

We should go to the circus, the woman said.

I haven't been to the circus in years. Not since school.

I'm working.

In my dream, my stomach turned to ice, my glass fell from my hand. I knew—I *know* with such brutal certainty—that my death occurs only two weeks after this conversation.

The doctor calls it depression. I disagree.

When I drive to the beach and sit alone looking out to sea, or when I'm stretched out on a blanket in the park with a picnic and my friends, I feel happy. I *am* happy. When I listen to music, I dance and sing along. Would the doctor think me depressed if he saw me dancing around my kitchen?

I'm in limbo, though; I haven't found my place in the world. I'm not sure I *have* a place. What's the point of making plans when you won't be around to achieve them? What's the point of making the effort when the reward is impossible?

*

In the middle of the night, a couple of months later, when Will thinks I'm sleeping, he leaves me. He grabs the pre-packed bag from wherever he hid it and closes the door softly behind him. I sit up and switch on the light, hoping he looks back along the road and sees it. Sees that I know he's gone.

It's not the first time. I doubt it will be the last. In a few days', he'll knock on the door and shrug his shoulders, a pathetic apology not quite making it out of his mouth. And we'll start all over again.

***

I am twenty-seven tomorrow.

You'd think I'd be past having nightmares. But the older I get, the darker they become.

It's half-past five, an hour before my alarm. The sun is already filling the room with golden rays. My pink childhood teddy, Alfie, sits on his chair in the corner, watching over me. I resist the urge to pick him up and cuddle him close.

I yawn widely, exhausted after another restless night, and the dream drifting around my head. I should be used to it, but I still fear the shadows.

At half-six, the melody of the wind chime alarm bursts out of my phone, and I start the day with indifference. I'll glide through it being the person I ought to be, work with a smile on my face, and spend the evening in the pub with friends.

There was a point I considered a better job, a different town, but I'm settled enough—I don't need more. When I was with Will, he'd talk about marriage and children, and I went along with it. If he wanted a better job, I'd have supported him; if he wanted to move, I'd have followed. I guess there was a moment when he suspected I was going through the motions of existing, when his 'where do you want to be in five years?' conversations didn't pan out the way he planned.

He didn't leave. I pushed him away.

After that, I decided I was better off alone. I've learnt how not to scare friends off, but romance and settling down are for other people—people who expect to stay alive.

I shower and eat breakfast as quietly as possible so as not to disturb my flatmate Niall, who works at the Boatman and sleeps until mid-morning. I dress. I drop my dishes in the sink for later. In a flash, in a blur, I'm at work. Clare, standing beside the giant recycling bins having a sneaky cigarette, greets me. "You look terrible."

"Didn't sleep."

"Again? You need tablets."

"I'm fine. I don't need anything."

She stubs out the cigarette and follows me inside. Coat on hook, bag in locker, corporate mug ready to be filled with strong coffee. I look around but it's all so pointless. I'm weighted to the floor.

"Pub?" Luisa says at the end of the day.

It's not a question any-more; it's so regular we grab our things and assume it's the direction we'll be headed.

Along the road, down the steep hill, turn and turn again. The river is grey this evening, but calm. I slow down and I'm last to enter the pub, drawn as always by the striking view downstream, and the soporific swish of the tide against the small beach. Overhead, a train rumbles along the bridge into town.

Jake's at the bar buying the first round, chatting easily to Niall. They've known each other for years; it's that kind of town. I knew them both at school without realising—Niall was in a drama club with me, and Jake was in my history A-level class when I was too busy failing it to notice who I was sitting next to.

When the drinks arrive, I glance around the table: Jake, Clare, me, Luisa. The four of us. A formless thought rises, floating like cigarette smoke. I take a gulp of lager and feel the fizz of bubbles bouncing around my mouth. The four of us sitting here, with glasses on the table. A nudge; a lingering feeling.

The four of us together. These glasses on the table, Niall at the bar, the music—the brand-new chart topper I've heard for years. But this is different; this isn't my dream. How did I not notice before? The bracelet on my wrist, my favourite orange shirt. When did I buy these things? Why didn't I stop myself?

The dream and the reality fold together. Something needs to change before it's too late and the shape of the dream takes hold.

I stand abruptly. "Who fancies a bottle of wine?" There's never a bottle on the table. A bottle could change everything.

Clare shakes her head. Luisa looks at her glass and says, "Nah, I'm okay with this."

"So, what's this year's birthday wish?" Jake asks before I can press the point any further.

Still standing, I try to catch Niall's attention to mime my order. He's serving someone. I sit. I'll buy it in a minute. "To get a decent night's sleep, I suppose." I grin, but it's not a joke. I glance at the bar. He's moved to another customer.

"No," they chorus. Clare adds, "A proper wish. You must *want* something. Winning the lottery or snagging your dream job? The guy from the deli on the corner?"

I laugh. "Yeah, all of that." I half stand again. "But, right now, I really fancy some wine..." Luisa pulls me back into my chair. I comply with a sigh, with another distracted glance towards the bar.

"What are we doing for your birthday?" Jake asks.

"We should go to the circus," Clare says, without warning, without prelude.

Before I can stop him, Jake says, "I haven't been to the circus in years. Not since school."

His voice is muffled and diluted.

"I'm working," says Luisa with a frown.

She's drifting away; her features are dissolving in front of me.

I drop my glass. Or Jake removes it from my hand. I stare in horror, from one friend to the next, unable to put my panic into words. Their faces are puzzled and concerned. I can't breathe;

I'm clammy and queasy. I'm cold, shivering violently. I'm inside the dream. The previously murky details spring into sharp focus.

And so, it begins. The end, apparently.

My end.

Breathe in...

Breathe out...

***

I am twenty-seven years old. Today.

It's two in the morning; the night is as dark as it's going to get. I'm awake. I haven't slept. Stupid. What am I afraid of? It occurs to me I'm not afraid. I'm relieved. It's not a dream anymore. Not a random event hanging over me. I'm going to die. But it's okay.

Relieved, but a little sad, a little regretful. I could have done more with the life I had. Twenty-seven is old enough to have fitted things in—almost ten years of adulthood. Some people don't even get that. I should have travelled, volunteered to build schools in African villages, worked with kids in deprived areas; I could have helped, made a difference.

Too late now.

I'm twenty-seven years and two hours old, and I've wasted my life.

We should go to the circus.

I didn't even know the circus was in town. If I'd seen a poster, I might have suspected earlier. I'm embarrassed it came as such a shock; I thought I was ready.

Imagine you're looking forward to a holiday. You found the perfect destination, chosen the best resort, booked it—but it's not until next year. You've got months to wait. You go to work, get on with your life, pick up new bikinis in the January sales. And then, finally, it arrives. The day you go on holiday. Imagine your delight.

That's how I feel. This thing I've been expecting is here. Maybe I'm not anticipating it with comparable excitement, but instead with a tumultuous, restless energy.

I fall asleep as the sun rises. I don't dream. My head is black and empty, and I sleep better than I ever have. When I wake to the commotion of Niall accepting a delivery, I recall the wish Jake pressed me to make. I must remember to tell him it came true.

Niall knocks on my door and enters with a large bouquet of flowers. "Delivery for the birthday girl. From your parents." He lays it on my bed and hands me several cards. "Happy birthday."

I yawn and stretch and start opening the envelopes. One from Niall, one from Mum and Dad, a couple from old uni friends who keep in touch.

"Are you okay this morning? Were you ill?"

"No, it was nothing. Honestly," I add when he doesn't appear convinced.

"Well, I'm off to work in a mo. Have a good day. Phone if you need me. Will you be coming down later?"

"I expect they'll drag me out for a couple."

"Are you going to the circus?"

I wince. "Um, I don't think so. I'm not keen on them, really."

After he's gone, once solitude is assured, I take the flowers into the kitchen to find a vase. We don't have one—I'm twenty-seven and don't own a vase—so I fill a bucket with water and leave them in there.

I start to think of all the things I should do if I've only got two weeks left. The skinny-dipping and sky-dives and all-night raves I could attend.

I think of the things I'd like to tell my boss, the truths I *really* want to impart. Because I'll be dead soon, why the hell do I need a job?

I think of all the blokes I could sleep with—fourteen days, fourteen men? I start to make a list but stop when I realise what I'm doing and how inappropriate it is.

Saturdays are the perfect day for a birthday. The Boatman is lively, and we sit in the glorious sunshine in the patioed beer garden beside the water, my harbingers and I. We sip drinks and eat pizza from the van that sets up nearby and comment it's like the height of summer despite it being almost September. Kids are paddling in the river and jumping from the jetty. On the green further across, people are sunbathing and enjoying ice creams. The river is teeming with boats and paddleboarders.

We talk easily and lightly about nothing of consequence, and I know they're trying to avoid mentioning last night. Clare took me home and made me a mug of tea—making sure I was okay before leaving me alone—but aside from that, my memory is foggy.

I place my glass on the table and lean forward. They stop talking; I have their attention.

"I want to explain about yesterday," I say and stop. Because *how* do I explain? "I've had the same dream for years and years, ever since I was a little kid. A nightmare, really. A premonition, I think."

Now what? Do I carry on? It's not too late to finish off with a lame joke which will have them irked because they thought I was going to say something important.

They're waiting, all eyes on me.

"It always starts with Clare saying we should go to the circus like she did yesterday. And it ends, this dream, two weeks later... when I... when I die."

There's silence, then collectively, they break into uncomfortable laughter.

"Oh, Ella. I thought you were going to be serious."

"Shit, you had me going for a moment, though."

Jake is quiet. I catch a peculiar look in his eye, and he glances away quickly.

I smile weakly and say nothing because there's nothing to say. No one comments further; they move on as if I'd said nothing at all. I'm overlooked, ignored, embarrassed.

"I'm getting another drink." I don't wait for their responses.

Inside, it takes a moment for my eyes to adjust to the dimness. There's a composure to the conversation in here, muted and relaxed, whereas outside is full of shrieks and exuberance.

"Niall says it's your birthday. Happy birthday," Rona says as I reach the bar.

"Thank you."

"Lovely day for it. What can I get you? This one's on the house, Chris's treat."

I nod towards the landlord. "Cheers, Chris. I'll have a cider."

While Rona pours, I glance at the mirror behind the bar and don't recognise myself. The edges of me are warped, my expression blank. Perhaps I'm already fading away.

"Are you okay? You don't seem yourself."

"It's been a long twenty-seven years." I smile. It's a joke, please laugh. But she doesn't. She considers me with more gravity than my friends did.

When I reach for my pint, she takes my hand. "If you need to talk, I'm always here."

"Um, thank you. But I'm fine. You take stock, don't you? Ageing makes you think."

She nods, smiles, and moves to the next customer.

Our table is filling up when I return. That's what happens when you make friends; you accumulate others. Clare's partner and her sister have arrived. Luisa's husband is here, and several people who are their friends more than mine but I don't mind hanging out with have turned up too. They've spilled onto other tables. It makes it a party now. A birthday party. They cheer when I push through the melee, and I'm hit with a chorus of 'Happy Birthday'.

The afternoon progresses into evening. As the air cools, people make their way inside. I'm gathering a few glasses to take back to the bar when Jake appears behind me, his hands circling my waist.

"Come with me," he says, taking the glasses from me and putting them back down. He leads me to the low wall separating the beach from the beer garden.

The tide's in, reflecting the pub's lights in a way that feels quite magical. I sway with the movement and briefly touch the railings to centre myself.

"Ella."

He stops and opens his mouth a couple of times, tentative and nervous. He sits on the wall and twists himself so he's facing the river.

"I can't believe I'm going to ask you this... Do you really believe it, what you said, about your dream? About dying?"

He catches me off-guard. "Oh, wow. Um, yes, I think so." I sit beside him and all the things I've wanted to share with someone suddenly evaporate. I take a moment to get the words in the right order. "I've had the same dream ever since I was little. Vague to start with, but more and more vivid as I got older. You were always there, and Clare and Luisa. But I didn't *know* it was you until..." I see a black hole in front of me, a vacuum; my fate. "It would be foolish to ignore it."

"It isn't coming true, you know. It's *just* a dream." His voice is harsh, almost angry.

"Everything happened last night the way it does in my dream. Every single word, the music playing, the number of glasses on the table. How do *you* explain it?"

He grasps my wrists with both hands. "People don't have premonitions about stuff like this. They don't have premonitions at all! It's nonsense, Ella."

"Well, if I'm dead in a fortnight, you'll know I was telling the truth."

"How can you make stupid jokes like that?" He lets go of me.

I bow my head, sober and serious despite the alcohol in my system, matching Jake's demeanour. "I can't explain it. I *know*, deep down—like knowing my left hand is doing this." I raise my hand to his face, pausing when I touch his cheek.

He reaches up to cover my hand with his own. A rush of voices carries on the breeze, and we both draw back.

"I hate that these thoughts have been in your head for so long."

"But look what happens when I tell people."

He pulls me into a hug, wrapping his arms tightly around me and resting his chin on the top of my head. When I try to stand back, he offers only a little leeway. He stares at me for a moment, then kisses me; a soft kiss, a whispered kiss. I lean in further, but he stands back in confusion.

"We should go inside. They'll be wondering where we are." He strides away, leaving me baffled. I watch him disappear into the pub and turn back to the river, hand over my mouth to retain the shock. I am twenty-seven years and twenty-one hours old, and I still don't know what to do when a man kisses me.

A swish of oars distracts me as I turn to walk away. It's dark on the river, with nothing but shadows from the bridge above and the twinkle of lights. I listen to the rhythmic sound for a moment, scanning for the boat. The water is undisturbed in all directions; perhaps it's the wind I can hear.

I stand at the door and watch my friends enjoying themselves. If I'd gone to volunteer in Africa, I wouldn't know these people. I wouldn't have been here last night. Clare wouldn't have suggested going to the circus.

By accepting this as my destiny, have I caused it?

I could have been a thousand miles away, sipping sangria in Spain, married to someone amazing, not giving a second thought to the dreams that would forever remain childhood nightmares.

All this time, I persuaded myself my future was an immovable outcome; yet I had the power to prevent it. And now it's too late.

Someone puts a drink in my hand. I look up and smile at Dean, a bloke who hangs around with us sometimes. Also, by chance, one of the names on the list I made earlier. But that's irrelevant—Dean usually has a girlfriend in tow, although never the same one for more than a few months.

"Happy birthday."

"Hello. Thank you." I sip the drink and frown. I hold the glass up to him. "What the hell?"

"Orange juice, sorry. Niall said you'd been here for most of the day, so he's cut you off."

"Just when I thought I was a grown-up..."

"I can get you something else."

"No. He's probably right, but don't tell him." I hold a finger to my mouth. *Sssh.* "So, where's... your girlfriend tonight?" I search for a name, but it escapes me.

He smiles. "We broke up."

"Too bad." I move to sit down on a nearby stool. I launch myself onto it but misplace my foot and fall forward into Dean's chest. "Oops. Strong orange juice."

His hand flew out to catch me, and it remains on my waist. My mind propels forward and imagines his kiss, his touch, his body against mine.

"Maybe it's time to think about going home. I'm walking your way if you..." he says as if reading my mind. A hand on my waist, the other gesturing towards the door.

Niall watches closely. He does that—keeps an eye on me, takes his role of flatmate, protector, substitute brother seriously. I love him for it. I wish he could always be there to keep me safe. But not tonight. Tonight, I don't want to be safe.

My eyes are sealed shut; my head spins. Daylight streams through the open curtains. My limbs are numb. My mouth dry. I try to sit up, but my head spins and I slump back down. Outside, the usual sounds of Sunday morning force themselves into my consciousness. Too early. In fact, tomorrow would be too early. I roll over, which makes my nausea worse, so I stagger into the kitchen for water.

"Morning. I'm making scrambled egg if you want some." Niall darts from the hob to the fridge, grabbing ingredients, preparing his feast.

"Uh. No."

I sit at our bistro table, and he miraculously produces coffee.

"Loverboy left, if you're wondering."

"Who? Oh, shit. Dean." Head in hands, the pulsing headache pauses to allow space for my embarrassment. "Did we...?" Everything is hazy.

"How should I know?"

"Are you cross with me?"

He says nothing. He sets his breakfast on the table and searches for cutlery. "What you get up to is none of my business."

"Exactly." I nod. He nods. I stare at my mug and steel myself for another sip, waiting for the sickness to abate. I watch Niall cut his toast and scoop the egg. I watch his hands. I remember Dean's hand on my waist.

There are hands in my dream—hands that push me. Whose hands? Who pushes me? I never see the face; I barely discern a body beside me. But someone must be there. Hands don't push by themselves.

As quickly as the thought rises, it evaporates. It doesn't really matter, does it? I rest my head back against the wall, close my eyes, and listen to the homely sounds of Niall finishing his breakfast and tidying up. He leaves the room without a word, and I stare at the space he's left with remorse.

I rest my arms on the table and flop my head down on top of them. Why does all of this feel so wrong? My phone rings while I'm in the middle of a low-pitched wail. Jake.

"I'm sorry about last night," he says immediately.

"Sorry?"

"About kissing you."

He kissed me? Of course he did. We were outside. I remember. It was quite nice. Then I slept with someone else. Okay. Should I regret something? If so, which thing?

"I wondered if you'd like to go for a drink?"

"Coffee would be nice, and some fresh air. I'm never actually drinking again."

On this beautiful morning, we decided to meet at the coffee kiosk across the green from the Boatman, but I'm early so I walk on.

The tide is on its way out. Soon, the small boats moored near the shore will be stranded on the silt. The creek, just off the river, will be devoid of water altogether.

When I reach Millers Bridge, I look up in awe. It's a tall, grey-stoned viaduct, centuries old, with five majestic arches spanning the creek. Within those arches, intricate Victorian brickwork always draws my eye. I shudder as a breath of air rushes past me. I close my eyes and listen for the ghosts.

It was originally called Knott's Viaduct—and probably still is, on maps and in official documents, but locally it's been known as Millers Bridge since Helen, daughter of a prominent landowner, died here in 1874.

Helen was in love with the ferryman who took passengers across the river, but she was engaged to the local magistrate, who her father had selected for political reasons. Helen and her ferryman planned to elope, but her father discovered the scheme and killed the ferryman on the evening they were due to leave town. When Helen discovered he was dead, she threw herself from the half-constructed viaduct in despair.

Everyone who grows up in this town knows the story. The day you start at the secondary school, the older kids gather you up and tell you the story. They act it out, wallowing in every tiny detail, enhancing the horror. *Their ghosts*, the kids whisper, *roam the riverside searching for each other*. They'll say, *if you listen carefully, you can hear her scream.*

The older kids tell you this because they know the first homework assignment you do for art is to draw the bridge. Only the bravest of eleven-year-olds does that homework alone.

I lean forward, listening for her screams. The wind circling the pillars creates an eerie, disorientating wail. My gaze tracks up, up, up, following the evenness of the stonework, the perfection of the arches. It's a long way; no wonder her scream hasn't ended. I hear a whisper, a jumble of words on top of each other, as though many people are talking all at once.

A hand brushes my shoulder. I yelp and spin around.

Jake!

I catch my breath and feel my heart racing. He laughs at my panic, then clasps both of my shoulders. "Are you okay?"

"You scared the hell out of me." I push him away and turn slowly on the spot, trying to alleviate my embarrassment. This is an awkward enough meeting without making a fool of myself in this way. "I was listening for the screams. You remember—from school?"

He laughs again. "That old story? The landowner's daughter and the ferryman. I scared a few Year 7s with that one, I can tell you." He stops and considers me. "You were freaked out by that?"

"No. Of course not."

"Come on, let's get a coffee. We probably ought to talk." He beckons me to join him.

"That sounds ominous."

"I kissed you."

"I know. But... what's there to talk about? It didn't mean anything, did it? We're friends, and..."

"Have you never thought we could be more?"

"Your timing's not great."

"Your dream," he says with incredulity.

"And." And Dean. I have to tell him about Dean. *Dean* will probably tell him about Dean. "I slept with Dean last night." I stare at the pavement. We've stopped walking. "I was drunk. He walked me home."

He emits a bitter laugh. "Great."

"You didn't mean anything by it. You *phoned* me to apologise."

"Only because... And it was after you went home with—" he gestures effusively, unable to say Dean's name. "So, you wouldn't have known if I'd meant it or not."

"Did you?"

"I don't know. But it would have been nice to have had time to think about it."

He doesn't wait for a response. He stomps back along the road and out of sight, leaving me in the shadow of the bridge. For a moment, I feel someone standing beside me.

***

I am twenty-seven years and two days old, and I'm going to die soon. I feel the profound sadness, the immeasurable loss. When I wake up, I have tears running down my face and onto my pillow.

It's dark. Four or five o'clock on Monday morning. Is this what death feels like—existing in the half-light between night and day forever? Quiet and stagnant, staring at the ceiling? I don't want to die. But I don't have the choice. My fate is mapped out in front of me, waiting.

And just when I need friends around me, I'm pushing them away. What did Jake mean he *didn't know* if he meant anything by kissing me? How does anyone not know something like that? He's always been serious, always sitting back and thinking and considering. Even in my dream, before it was him, he had that air about him. I picture him considering all the pros and cons of it even as he was leaning down towards me.

I *know* I didn't mean anything by sleeping with Dean; it was a distraction, taking the edge off my swirling, endless thoughts.

The sky brightens, birds sing from the rooftops. Another day begins. Another day closer. I'm scared for the first time. I'm too young. I fumble for my phone and find my mum's number. No, Dad's. No, neither. What would I say? They moved away five or six years ago, when I was leaving uni and coming home. Turns out there wasn't going to be a home to come back to. It put a dampener on our relationship. They think sending money and bouquets of flowers on my birthday and at Christmas is enough. They visit once a year, or I go to them. We scrape around for topics to talk about, for things we might still have in common, and it so happens there isn't much. Each time, we leave our visits a little longer. How would that conversation go?

I drop the phone onto the floor and let my arm dangle over the side of the bed until the tingle of pins and needles sets in.

A flash and a blur, and I'm at work. A flash and a blur, and I'm walking home. The time in between passes without me realising. Is that how easily the hours and days slip away? Is that how the next two weeks will transpire? How the end of my days will be upon me so readily?

It's raining—not hard enough to run for cover under the nearest shop awning and wait it out with three other people and a Labrador, but hard enough that I'll be drenched when I get home.

"Hey, Ella!" Dean waves from the other side of the road and darts around the slow rush hour traffic to reach me.

"Hi."

"Um, yeah, hi." He laughs self-consciously, as though not quite sure what to do next. "I'm sorry for leaving without saying goodbye yesterday."

"Oh, no..." My hand waves dismissively.

"I had to—"

"No, it's fine."

He looks along the road and then back at me. Rain drips from his fringe; he blinks the water away. "Are you free for a drink sometime? Or now maybe?" Another nervous laugh. "We could grab something to eat?"

"I've got to get out of these clothes."

"Oh, yeah, of course. Another—"

"You could always come to mine if you like. We could order a pizza."

His smile makes me quiver; tender, and oh so sexy. "Sure."

Home is a ten-minute walk away, so we're both soaking when we arrive.

"I'm going to change. I'll get you a towel. I can lend you a T-shirt if you need it. Niall might have something."

"The towel is fine."

I peel off my wet clothes and swap them for a shapeless top and baggy jeans. I don't want to look as though I'm trying; I want to appear casual and comfortable, the way I would if any of my friends popped round like this.

We share a pizza, and I find bottles of lager in the fridge.

"How was the hangover?"

"Not too bad, in the end. Lots of coffee saw me right." I fight with the cheese looping itself across my fingers, then sit silently to contemplate my next statement. "I have a bit of a confession." I grimace when he looks up with interest. "I don't exactly remember what happened on Saturday. I know you walked me home." I shove my fist against my mouth to prevent further words from sliding out. That was probably enough for a man's ego to take.

He smiles slyly. "Oh. Really." He puts down a half-eaten slice, looks as though he's going to explain, then picks up his lager. He swigs. I wait. He swigs again. I hold my breath. "Nothing happened. You were *rather* inebriated, so I tucked you in and slept on your extremely uncomfortable armchair. Well, not exactly slept. That's why I left so early. I needed my bed!"

"Oh." I blush and think of all the nice things people have ever done for me. "Thank you." In all the time I've known Dean, his random flitting in and out of our circle of friends, I'm not sure it's what I expected of him.

Our conversation flows more easily. We have another lager; I open a tub of ice cream. I find myself moving closer and closer to him, and then I kiss him.

With Dean breathing softly beside me and his arm heavy across my stomach, I stare at the ceiling and notice cracks I haven't seen before. I see shapes and trace patterns in the uneven plaster. I see a bridge, and a woman, and the river and a rowing boat coursing towards her.

And then I'm on the bridge, standing at the edge, peering over at the dark water below. The tide is going out. As the waves ebb, it's possible to see the silty sand and deep ridges carved into it.

Not yet, says a voice.

Both Helen and I look around, but no one's there. It's just the two of us. She smiles sadly and holds out her hand. When I reach for it, she moves quickly and her hand is on my back, pushing, pushing with all her might.

I jump awake. Dean stirs and rolls over, facing away from me. I pull the duvet up and curl myself around him, feeling his heart beating and his chest rising and falling. The rhythm is enough to help me find mine, and I fall back to sleep.

When I open my eyes again, Dean's sitting on my chair.

"Sneaking out again?"

"I was going to wake you," he whispers, leaning over to kiss my forehead. "I have to go home before work and get changed."

"Oh."

"It was a great night. Unexpected." He waits for a reply, but I don't know what to say.

"Do you want something to eat before you go? Coffee?"

"No, I'll get something at home. But I'll phone you, yeah?

I smile and nod. "Sure. We'll probably bump into each other at the pub anyway."

"Or... we could go out one evening. The cinema maybe?" Shirt on, trousers on, socks and shoes.

"Like a date?" I blurt out, then mentally kick myself.

"Yeah, a date."

A date is more serious than a one-night stand. It leads to another date, and another, and to the expectation of cosy evenings in front of the TV and buying each other presents at Christmas. A date is the beginning of something, and if this had happened at any other point in my life, I'd have jumped at it. But now? Now I'd just be increasing the number of mourners at my funeral.

Dean shudders as he slips into his still-damp jacket and adjusts the collar. I stare at his hands. What would they feel like on the base of my spine, shoving me forward?

He sees himself out and I remain where I am, hiding from the day ahead.

Work anchors me, gives me something mundane and repetitive to focus on. I fell into this job by accident, but it's as good as any. By accident or by fate? If I hadn't got this job five years ago, I wouldn't have met Clare three years ago or Luisa when she joined last spring. We wouldn't be friends who go to the pub and organise each other's birthdays or suggest going to the circus together.

"Do you think it's possible to predict the future?" I ask Luisa as we collect our belongings from the staff room at the end of the day.

She peers over the top of her locker. "Are you still thinking about that silly dream?"

"Not *that* dream. All the dreams."

"People don't dream their own deaths."

"That's a myth, you know. I looked it up."

"Of course you did." She pauses. "Okay, but if they do, it doesn't mean they're all going to die."

"How do you know?" She looks quizzical, so I continue. "Say I had a dream and knew how I was going to die—which I have—but didn't tell you about it. And then, say, I died in the exact same way I dreamt. But"—I stab my forefinger into the air—"you don't know about the dream, so you don't know I predicted it, and I can't tell you... because I'm dead."

I smile victoriously, my point succinctly and well made.

"Okay. Say you're right and you do know. Surely the *fact* you know means you can prevent it. It hasn't happened yet. What if it's one of many things that could happen?"

"But I've tried. The dream adapts."

Luisa nods emphatically. "Exactly! Because the future isn't set. It changes. You're not going to die. This is all impossible."

"But—"

"Ella, look. We're worried about you. We want to help, but..."

"You can't help!" We're out on the road, about to head in our separate directions. Both of us are baffled as to how a genial conversation has led me to raise my voice.

"Ella?" She reaches out to touch my arm.

Her hand... Ready to push?

"Get off me!" I spring away from her. "Leave me alone."

I hurry away. Someone pushes me. Who? Maybe they all do. They all want me dead. Luisa and Clare and Jake and Niall, and even Dean. Because why would he suddenly be hanging around? Why else would he be wheedling his way into my life?

Dean? Of course. It makes the most sense.

Or it makes no sense, and I'm tired of it all.

When I reach the flat, I thunder inside and lock the door behind me. I lean against it and slide to the floor, catching my breath, planning what to do next.

I pack a bag, stuffing it until it's overflowing with clothes and toiletries and the salad dressing I adore but Niall hates and the kettle after I've emptied it, of course. I search for other things I might need. A knife for protection against those hands; the photo of a mother and baby giraffe because I like it.

The flowers my parents sent for my birthday are wilting in the bucket because I haven't topped up the water. I could go to them. I'd be safe there. No one would know me.

"What are you doing?"

I open my eyes and Niall is towering above me. I'm lying on the floor, my over-full bag acting as a pillow. All the useless items I was trying to pack before I fell asleep are scattered around me.

"You're leaving?"

It takes me a moment to become coherent. I yawn and stretch, slowly sitting upright. "I've got to, haven't I? If I stay here…"

"You're not in any state to go anywhere." He's rooting through the bag. "What have you got my school football trophy for?"

I don't remember taking it. None of these things make sense, although they did.

"This is silly. I'm calling the doctor."

"No, please."

"I don't know how to help you."

I stare at him for a long time, considering all the things I could say, *ought* to say. They won't come out right; they'll jumble themselves and I'll be tied up in things I don't mean. I watch his expression altering with every passing second, his face reflecting each thought as it occurs to him. I want him hug me, but when I look at his hands, I involuntarily move away. And the only thing that makes sense is, "I don't want to die."

*

Days and nights; dreams and nightmares. We sit at a table—Clare, Luisa, Jake, and I. We drink, we talk and laugh, we stockpile our glasses. *We should go to the circus.*

Dean sleeps heavily next to me. How long has he been here? How many days? The more I gaze at his shape beneath the duvet, the more detached I feel. I close my eyes. I open them and he's not there. The pillow hasn't been used.

I wake, dripping with sweat; breathless as if I was drowning. A hand rests on the base of my spine, a caress at first.

A thick mist rolls in from the river, bringing a chill and a faint muddy smell with it.

I'm climbing up the side of a steep, grassy embankment.

I'm not in my own body.

These dreams and nightmares won't leave me alone.

***

It's Monday again, which means there are just six days until my untimely and violent death.

On the way to work, I detour towards residential roads which look down on Millers Bridge. I sit on the handy little bench someone has installed, and from here, it doesn't seem imposing at all. It looks like a model, a toy; something harmless and manageable. While I sit there, a train trundles across.

I watch the sun glistening on the water, deep azure blue under the vibrant sky. I watch the next train, and the next. When I check my phone, it's almost eleven o'clock and I've got three messages and a missed call from Clare. The tide reaches its high point. I wonder if Helen waited for the tide before she jumped, if she'd listened to her ferryman lover when he talked of the dangers of setting out at the wrong time and the strict routes he needed to take. Deeper water would surely mean a kinder end.

The messages are stacking up on my phone: Luisa, Jake, Dean. Word has got around I'm AWOL, I assume. They'll be discussing me, contemplating my precarious state of mind. Reprimanding themselves for not following through with the idea of calling for me and escorting me to work.

Work! Like I care about that anymore. It's far too late to care about work.

They don't understand I'm no longer in control, that Clare has forced this path upon me with her reckless words. Her fault, not mine. The conversations between them will be increasingly frantic. So many people who care; so many hands awaiting the final push.

"Ella, please open the door."

When I came home, I avoided Niall, avoided the questions he would invariably ask. I hid in my room and waited until he left for work. But as he did, Luisa arrived. She stayed until he returned at half-past midnight, and after lunch, when he was preparing to leave again, Clare arrived.

They're babysitting me, crossing paths with each other so I won't be alone—and therefore won't be able to abscond—and no one will have to press the buzzer, which I could ignore. *Would* ignore.

Now it's Luisa again. I imagine she's sitting on the floor outside my bedroom, leaning against the wall with her legs crossed. Or perhaps she dragged a chair from the kitchen. She's brought fish and chips with her; I can smell the vinegar and grease.

"Niall says you're not eating. Would you like to share mine? There's enough for two. Hmm, it's delicious. Just open the door a bit and you can grab some."

Her presence is comforting with the door between us, but I can't face her.

"Everyone's been asking after you," she says lightly. "But we're not sure what to say."

Don't say anything. Leave me alone.

"Open the door, Ella. Please talk to me."

There's a rustle as she chases her chips around the polystyrene tray. My mouth waters. It's not that I'm not eating—I've got bars of chocolate and a bag of grapes here with me—I just can't get to the kitchen without confrontation.

"Are you even in there? Or am I talking to myself?" She laughs a little, light and frivolous, although I can hear the uncertainty in her voice.

I place my hands on the door, palms flat against the Victorian panelling. I want her hands to be mirroring mine on the other side. *Please help me.* Yet I prevent myself from saying it out loud.

A flash and a blur, and I'm twenty-seven and twelve days old. So close. Still holed up in my room, I can hardly bear the wait. And yet, if I'm here, I can't be there. If I remain hidden from everyone, my future alters. As simple as that. *Is* it as simple as that?

How does time work? How does the future reconcile itself with infinite possibilities? So many people, so many unique actions; each one having an extensive effect on not just one person, not ten, but on hundreds, thousands.

The only person I see is Niall. I have to leave my room periodically. I need to eat and visit the bathroom. A change of scenery, a different view from the window. I need to breathe different air.

"How are you doing?" he asks tenderly.

"Fine." I shrug and avoid catching his eye.

"I've made you an appointment with the doctor. I said I would, remember?"

"I don't need a doctor."

He wants to say something else but stops himself. He'll stop caring soon; I'll push him away. It's for the best. He won't grieve if he hates me. Or I might be turning him into the person who pushes me. A self-fulfilling prophecy, isn't that what they call it?

My sleep is deep and encompassing, the kind of blackness which becomes radiant and colourful as your eyes acclimatise. My body acquiesces to the weightlessness, to the movement, to the hands which hold me. I dream I'm walking along the riverbank, then swimming through the dark water. Then I'm gliding on top of it, steered by the strong arms of the ferryman, becoming part of the river as I lie on the surface and slowly lowered by those same arms.

"Helen, my love," he says.

I struggle away from him, and he's gone. We are both gone from the river. I am nowhere. I feel a jolt, a push, and I'm floating and weightless in the radiant colours of the night.

It's still dark when I open my eyes, content, almost relaxed. It's today. It happens today. And I'm not scared. Not anymore.

The sky is clear, the stars are immense. I sit by the window and watch them twinkle. For thousands of years, people have observed these same stars, creating stories and mythology to explain them, using them as a source of hope, a method of prediction. A thousand years ago, someone might have been sitting in this very same spot, looking at these very same stars.

A hundred and fifty years ago, the ferryman and his beloved Helen might have looked up and been assured of their union.

I feel a hand on my shoulder.

The room is empty aside from me. Everyone's asleep. Niall in his room. All the people in the houses along this road, and all the roads in town. I'm dressing before I realise it. I'm at the front door and closing it quietly behind me. I have no plan. I need to walk. I'm compelled to. The hand on my shoulder guides me.

I end up under Millers Bridge. All roads lead to it, eventually. To one side, if you fight through years of dense foliage and weeds tangled together, there's a steep access path to the railway line. Jake showed me once, years ago. It hasn't been fenced off. It really should have been.

In my dream, I've climbed this path and stood on the bridge, beside Helen or perhaps taken her place and become her. Is this a dream? I can no longer tell the difference. Am I in bed? Is Dean beside me, his arms wrapped around me to keep me safe?

I stand beside the old stone gatepost that marks the entrance and look all the way to the top. Poor Helen Miller, climbing here all those years ago, desperate in her grief. I feel her misery; I am choked in her anguish.

She stands before me, beckoning me to follow her. I don't want her to be alone anymore—it's been too long—so I take her hand. We squeeze ourselves up through the undergrowth, fighting past the nettles and trampling the dandelions. In front of me, Helen's skirts catch on the brambles, and she pauses to tug them free. When we reach the top, she smiles and fades into the soft mist rising from the river.

On each side of the viaduct is a low wall, no higher than mid-thigh. At regular intervals decorative railings cut in, rusted after so long in the elements. Below, there's nothing but blackness—no sense of the height or the path I've walked along to reach it. The water laps at the riverbank and the thick stone pillars of the bridge. On either side, the hills the train tracks disappear into are silhouettes against a sky that's paling with the approaching dawn.

I lean on the wall and peer over. A loose stone slips beneath my hand and I jump back, my heart racing. The bushes at the top of the path rustle and a figure emerges. It could easily be the ferryman come looking for his love, but it's not, of course.

"It's you." *You're the one who's going to push me.*

Jake stands a little uncertain, a little bashful. "Hey."

"What are you doing here?"

He digs his hands into his pockets. "I followed you."

"How...? When...?" I don't need to know—it's irrelevant. It's just me and Jake at the top of the bridge where it all ends.

"What are you doing here, today of all days?"

"I was asleep. I don't know."

"You should be at home."

I shrug. *I was. I thought I was,* but it doesn't matter anymore. "All my life has been leading to this moment. I was never meant to live a long and wonderful existence. It ends."

"No, it doesn't have to." He walks forward, stumbling a little on loose masonry. "Come on. Let's go back down and we can talk. We can talk all night if you want to."

"Like we used to."

He's standing close enough for me to see his smile. "Yeah, like that. Did you know I was in love with you? That that kiss on your birthday was a weak moment I'd been fighting for a long time?"

"You never said."

"It was never the right moment."

"You could have said."

"And now you're with Dean." He bows his head. The creeping indigo of dawn lines the horizon.

"Have you told the others where we are?"

"No."

Are you going to kill me because you're jealous?

I stare down; all the way down. The water ebbing below makes me dizzy.

"Let's go." He holds his hand out for me.

"It's my time. There's no point in running away, is there?"

"Of course there's a point. I'd be running so far away from this bridge. It's some random nightmare you've made into this huge *thing*." He spreads out his arms to show to extent of my supposed delusion. "You're so fucking melodramatic, you know that?"

"Well, thanks for the sympathy. You'll be leaving now?"

"No! Not without you. I'm not leaving you here to jump."

"I don't jump. I'm pushed."

We're both shouting. I wonder how far our voices carry; I wonder how audible our words are to the somnolent houses on the hills surrounding us.

"Well, let's get it over and done with then."

"What?"

"Well, you want to die, and I'm not doing anything else at the moment. I'll push you if it's what you want."

"I don't want to die. It's not about wanting or not wanting. It's going to happen anyway."

Jake's shoulders sag, the tension released. "You *don't* want to?" His voice is a whisper once more. He smiles, his face relaxes. He reaches for my hand again. "Then don't."

Our fingers entwine. I gaze down and can barely detect whose hand is whose.

He pulls on my arm, attempting to draw me back the way we both came. I hesitate. If only it were so easy—to follow Jake back down to the road, to walk with him until sunrise and start my life afresh.

I want to go with him. I want to walk away from all of this. But it's hard after so long believing something so deeply, so strongly. In my head, tomorrow doesn't exist. It never has.

I want to walk away, but something keeps me here, tugs me in the opposite direction. It shouldn't be a choice; I shouldn't even be here. What was I thinking? Jake was right. *Today of all days* I should be as far away from this bridge as possible.

"Okay," I say, my voice thin and far away, testing the word.

"Okay?"

I nod. "I want to go back down."

Jake's arm wraps around me as we shuffle back along the track to the break in the wall where the path begins. As it narrows, he goes first, testing the uneven rubble in the gloom. A stone shifts beneath me; I slide and instinctively reach for the wall to steady myself. The wall crumbles. I grab the railings, expecting a sturdy anchor, and it too shifts as I cling on to it. A hand on my back, a push from behind, causes me to lose my footing. My leg dangles over the edge; my other foot is caught on the metal.

"Jake!"

He spins in slow motion. I see the echo of his movement. And the terror on his face. I clamber, grapple, swing my leg to lever myself back up. Rough rust grinds into my palm.

"Don't look down. Look at me." He lies flat, his torso across the train track, and reaches out with both arms. "Take my hand."

The railings groan. My other leg slips away from me. I scream. "Help me!"

"I can't reach you."

The metal creaks. It cries. It bends further out over the side of the bridge. I flounder in mid-air.

With every movement, the railings lurch a little more. I'm going to fall. I know it; I've seen it. I'm going to let go. I can't hold on anymore. My fingers are bloody from the rusted metal digging into my hand.

"Ella!"

And then I'm flying, swooping through the air. Floating. The air buffets me. I feel a hand holding me, cradling me as if I were a baby.

Jake is smaller and smaller, up on the bridge. Such a long way away. He calls my name. I smile; I want him to know I'm going to be okay. I want him to know this is the most beautiful, the most peaceful I've ever felt. And then everything is dark, like the end of a dream.

OUR BEAUTIFUL CHILD

A wave of voices tumbles through the air and ebbs away. A glimmer of the past, a fragment of another time.

A ribbon of mist follows the curve of the river, receding as quickly as it formed. From this distance, it looks like the setting of a fairy tale, with buildings and lights stacked on top of each other on the steep hill. It looks like a dream.

Under Millers Bridge, Helen—the landowner's tragic daughter—wades through the water and pulls herself up onto the bank of the creek, as she's done countless times before. She sits in the shadows and waits patiently for her lover to find her, to collect the prize he never possessed in life. But this man—this boy, just a boy—is searching on the river half a mile away, on the tides by the Boatman where he was murdered.

In the large front room of a flat on Ashtorre Road, a lost soul paces back and forth, unable to comprehend what happened. A restless soul. The wound in his chest ceased to bleed long ago. Yesterday, they finally found his body, lying on the sofa, exactly as Quinn left him. The air was stale and rancid. The sound of water flowing in the kitchen was silenced. The sound that connected him to the living world gone. Murray watched as they reverently laid him in the black bag, zipped it up, and carried him out into the waiting van. The flat, abruptly busy and over-flowing with people, once again stagnant, unnerving.

He needs to be guided, taken under the wing of others who know the way. But he refuses to let them, averse to the world to which he now belongs. He bangs his head against the wall which, he's discovered, becomes fleetingly solid under his touch. It won't last long; the assumption of corporeality will subside. He pushes his weight against the sofa where he once sat, the stain a vivid red reminder. Pushing, pushing, and occasionally, he thinks it moves.

So many stories; so many souls. Every street corner and park, every house and office, factory or pub. We gather together, seeking each other out, craving solace. At the war memorial, with the perennial wreaths of poppies pulping and disintegrating, we are there as well.

We stand on Millers Bridge as the poor woman falls. Not Helen, this time, for she knew what she was doing when she jumped. No, this soul falls, struggles to hold on while her friend tries to reach her, strives to save her. But she can't, and he can't. He's helpless as she plummets, cries out when he hears the splash, so very far away. We're powerless as well; we have no authority to intervene. We wait with her. We hold her hand as she sinks to the bottom of the creek and slowly floats to the surface. We wait with her, on the bank of the river, while she tries to understand what's happening.

She shivers with the shock, with the chill of the water. She tries to call out to her friend on the bridge, but she's too far away.

She stares inquisitively at the body floating face down in the water.

"I knew I would die today," she says eventually, realising she still has a voice—though she carries such sadness we don't think she truly believed at all.

But look around you, we say*, you still exist. You've simply passed from one place to another. Dying is not the end.*

"I'm not cold anymore."

No. You're safe now.

We stroke her hair, hold her tight. The silence swirls around us; time falters. Already, she's retreating from the life she led, seeing it as someone else's. As the sun rises, they find the body, these people who have searched all night with torches and dogs. The call goes up; the group converges on the bank. Heads bowed, arms around one another, to witness the poor woman conveyed from the water.

Who's that, we ask? A man stands apart from the group, crying tears he doesn't wipe away. His arms hang heavily; his shoulders are hunched and defeated. When people talk to him, touching his arm to attract his attention, he lifts his head in confusion. He's the man from the bridge; the man who called out with such desperation.

She smiles a little, and a glow radiates around her. "Jake."

You can go and say goodbye if you like. We nudge her forward, nod our encouragement.

She stands beside him. She gazes deep into his eyes, a tear glistening on her cheek. She waits for him to notice her, but of course, he won't. For him, she's the body on the bank of the river with her skin a shade of grey. She reaches for his hand, for one last moment that is theirs alone. He squeezes his fist and looks directly at her, the briefest connection between that world and this. One she'll always remember.

***

Outside the Boatman, amongst the tables and chairs and giant umbrellas, a child of twenty-one called Rona watches the sun setting over the hills and houses on the opposite side of the river—a beautiful child trapped between this life and another. She watches the ferryman sweep his oars through the water with strength and grace, effortless, as if he's been rowing here for a lifetime. Which, of course, he has. A lifetime and more. Gliding silently without a ripple.

"Rona," Chris calls from the door, jolting her back to reality. "Hurry up with those glasses."

"Yeah, I'm coming." She hangs back, though, longing for the freedom of being out on the water tonight.

*

The Boatman collects misfits. Strange solitary creatures who yearn for contact with the outside world—but not too much. They sit, glass in hand, either staring at the table in front of them or gazing out of the window at some distant point on the horizon. While the other pubs in town offer cheap beer and wall-to-wall sports, here they find respite.

Rona sways between tables, lighting candles. Shadows hover on the walls, looming over the room; a slight menace, a slight disquiet prevailing. In the furthest corner, away from both the bar and the entrance, a candle refuses to be lit. A chill hangs on the air right at that spot. Rona relights it; it flickers as though a child is blowing it out. It goes out again, leaving a thin flume of smoke in its place.

A draught catches her, and she shivers. She feels the wooden floor beneath her feet; the thick stench of smoke fills her lungs. In the gloom, she sees the face of a man. He's staring intently at the table, his head moving slightly from side to side as though he's reading. But there's nothing on the table, nothing in his hands. Indeed, the more she looks, the more indistinct the outline of his body becomes.

He looks straight at her, his eyes wild and frightened. No, not *at* her. He looks past her, as though she's stepped in front of his actual target. The stare is ice cold. Rona feels a tightness around her neck. He disappears, leaving her gasping. His energy burns a little longer; the spot where he sat is outlined with a silvery glow.

"Oi, are you serving or what?"

Rona turns to the customer with relief. "Sure. Just a sec."

Carpet, fresh air, light. Music, the lilt of laughter, and the hum of chatter. It all returns. In the corner, there'd been silence. She glances back, noting with bafflement the flickering flame of the candle that had refused to light a moment ago.

"Cider," Chris says as Rona tidies the chairs and follows the last customer to the door. She locks it, shoving the large bolt into its catch. He's set three pints on the bar: for himself, Rona, and for Niall, who's wiping down and whistling softly.

Rona sits on a stool and swings her legs as she sips the cider—the best taste after a long and busy shift.

"You okay?" Chris asks.

"Yeah. Tired, that's all. Busy night."

"It's the weather—it brings everyone out and no one wants to go home again. We'll be back to just the regulars in a couple of weeks. It's calmer then. More time to breathe." He gulps his real ale and wipes his mouth with the back of his hand.

Rona watches Niall for a second. "How's he doing?"

"He won't talk about it. Weird business, though. Did *you* know Ella well? I saw you talking to her a few times."

"As much as I know anyone around here."

"You need friends."

"I like being on my own. It's less complicated."

"Sounds like there's a story to tell?"

Rona shakes her head. "Not really."

"So, when are you heading back to uni? We'll miss you."

"I'm not going anywhere." She rests her hands on the bar and pushes against it. "I've got nowhere to go and nothing to do."

"Don't... don't get stuck here. It's okay for the summer season, or for fitting in with something else. But... it's easy to settle." His tone is sincere and serious; he nods towards Niall, still whistling as he wipes the last table and blows out the candle. "People can lose themselves in a town like this."

Like Ella, she thinks. *Like the bloke who was staying in the room upstairs and ended up dead. So sad.*

"One day at a time. That's all I can manage right now."

"You're running away from something?"

She smiles weakly and takes another sip "No. Nothing as interesting as that."

Chris shrugs and smiles, though he knows there's more. He drains his glass. "Come on. Time to push off. You all right getting home, Ro?"

"Niall's walking with me." It's the same question and answer since she started working here a couple of months ago, but it's nice to have people looking out for her.

Outside, for a second, Rona loses sight of Niall. The wind stops blowing; she hears the clamour of horses' hooves. There *are* no horses, of course, though Rona looks behind her even so. As she turns, she hears a *Whoa, boy!* and the faintest outlines of a horse rears up on its hind legs, right on top of her. She gasps, cowering and crouching to the floor, almost shouting out. But the image evaporates as quickly as it appeared. Then there's silence again, an eerie vacuum. And the wind returns.

"Ro, hurry up. I haven't got all night."

"Coming."

She doesn't move straight away. She glances back towards the pub.

"Did you hear... did you just see... a horse?" The question is ludicrous, of course. She catches a glimpse of Niall's dubious expression and shakes her head, forcing herself to laugh. "Ignore me. I must be more tired than I thought. Home, James."

We choose her. We choose Rona. We hold hands in the darkness of the night sky and silently implore her to hear us.

***

Rona throws open her windows the next morning, basking in the gentle breeze that wafts through the flat. She wanders between her bedroom and the living room, trying to avoid the phone call she knows she must make.

A deep breath, a pensive frown, a glance towards her mobile on the table. She reaches for it and selects her mother's name.

"Hello."

"Rona, is that you? Oh, thank God. Where've you been? I've been so worried."

"I'm sorry."

"What's going on? The university rang me. They said you were missing."

"No, I'm not missing... I've left."

"*Left*?" Silence. Not even the sound of infuriated breathing on the end of the line. This is worse than she feared.

"Mum? Are you there?"

"Why? Why...? No. No... You haven't left. You're taking a break. You'll go back. You'll phone them and get this sorted. You're just taking some time out... going back in September. I'll phone them for you, get it..." There's panic in the woman's voice. The woman who is not listening.

"No, Mum. I've left for good. I hated it. I didn't want to go in the first place. I never wanted to. You expected it, so I thought I'd give it a go, see how it went. I tried." She grimaces at her words. Not lies, but not the truth either.

"But, Rona." Silence again. "You're throwing away your future. What will you do? How will you live? Where are you? I'll come and get you. We can sort this out face-to-face."

"There's nothing to sort out. I've got a job. I've found a little flat." She scrunches up her face. A lie. Two rooms and a bathroom. Her 'kitchen' is a worktop, with a tiny fridge and a portable hob. She can stand in her bedroom and touch opposite walls.

"A flat? That seems permanent." Sharp, perturbed.

"I needed somewhere to stay, that's all." She sighs. "I haven't made any decisions yet."

"Are you at least going to tell me where you are?"

"Cornwall."

"You're *not* going to tell me, are you?"

"It's a nice town. Small, friendly. I just need to be on my own for a bit. I'm fine. Everything's fine. I need some space."

"From me?"

"No, Mum. From myself, I think."

"You aren't making any sense."

"I know. But you trust me, don't you?"

Her mother emits a protracted sigh. "Of course I do. Cornwall, then. We used to go down there on holiday when you were small. Do you remember?"

"Yes. That's why I came here."

"Perranporth. That's where we used to go. Is that where you are?"

Rona shakes her head. "Mum..." A montage of childhood recollections floods her. "I'll phone soon. I promise. I just need some time."

***

Help me. Help me, please.

The full moon shines in the midnight sky, casting an ethereal light onto our dark town. Stars twinkle; Venus is resplendent. A boat pushes through the water on its nocturnal crusade. The rippling water is soft and melodic.

Here we are too, standing at the edge of the water, watching the ferryman as he tries to answer those entreaties. But it's not the ferryman's beloved, Helen, who's calling for help, it's Rona herself, and I am beside her, and neither of us is who we're supposed to be.

She wakes suddenly, breathing rapidly, her vibrant eyes full of terror. I am flung from her subconscious, from the dream that consumed us both, just as frightened and mystified. How did I end up there? That's never happened before.

Rona stares at me. *At. Me.* Mouth open, her hand reaching out to me; a scream swallowed. Then her focus shifts, and she scans the room. It's changed—her radio and light fittings have vanished, the canvas-covered clothes rail in the corner replaced by a sturdy oak cabinet. The partition wall between her bedroom and the other room has gone, and thick velvet curtains hang at the all the windows of the enlarged chamber. Several red upholstered Chippendale chairs line the edges of the room.

She pulls her duvet around her, up to her neck, comforted by its warmth and softness. Within seconds, her expression relaxes.

The room is as it should be again; the surroundings of the past have dematerialised.

I'm cold out here, exposed. It's been so long since I've felt anything, I relish the moment, but don't understand what's happening. I thought I knew all there was to know about this existence. Yet a moment ago we were back among *my* furniture and décor. A moment before that, I had the air on my skin. I tasted the river.

We return to the scene of our deaths, but we are not fixed there; we are not held captive by the walls and memories. We are not echoes of a previous time playing over and over like a broken reel of film. We return to draw strength, to remember who we once were. We return to connect with something solid and real.

We use the word *we* because *I* starts to diminish at the point of death. We are a river where individual raindrops remain perfectly formed—our memories remain, but our attachment to them deteriorates.

Since Rona arrived in town, this life is fracturing. *I* is returning. We do not understand. I've been embraced and surrounded all these years, and yet I'm becoming more and more isolated.

***

Later, days or weeks perhaps—time drips so slowly—the sun is hazy and fatigued as the summer draws to an end.

Jane Markham holds her head high and marches along the road—a woman in control, a woman with purpose. She checks her watch—precisely quarter to twelve—and steps through the door of the Boatman. She jolts. There's a discernible chill in the air which she attributes to ghosts and spirits rather than the fact the building is constructed from granite and has sat in place for over four hundred years. And, indeed, who am I to disagree?

"We're shut," says a voice before she can see a person.

"I'm sorry?" Movement behind the bar causes her to pivot on the spot. "Mr Cookson?" She holds out her hand. "Jane Markham."

"Er, right. Hello."

"You're expecting me. I phoned yesterday," she prompts with a terse tone.

"Oh, right. Jane. Yes, of course. Chris. Call me Chris." He looks down at his own hand, wipes it on his jeans, and belatedly offers it forward. She smiles with a hint of revulsion and withdraws. "So, um, this is the Boatman," he says through lack of anything else to say. "Have you been here before?"

She sweeps her eyes around, notes the worn seat covers, the dust gathering in dark corners, the slight crispness of the carpet. She settles upon him again, her lips slightly pursed. "No, Mr Cookson, I haven't. Although, I have read about the supernatural activity you experience here. Which, of course, is why I contacted you."

"I never really think of it like that. Just shadows, isn't it? An old building settling itself. Hardly anything at all, really."

"The *sightings*, Mr Cookson. *Sixteen* in the past two years?"

"Sixteen isn't many." He stops and swallows nervously. "Is it?"

"Well, yes, it is rather a lot." She narrows in with piercing blue eyes. "Have you seen anything yourself?"

He hesitates. "Well, I... I guess... No... Maybe. I don't know. Sometimes I look up quickly, or open a door, and I think maybe there's something there. I never see anything properly. I mean, ghosts aren't real. It's people's imagination running wild in old buildings." He starts to stack beer mats on the bar.

"Hmm, I see."

"Of course, it's my bar lass you really ought to speak to. She has a bit of a knack for stumbling across strange things. She'll be in soon, if you want to wait."

"A *knack*?" She smiles condescendingly. "Very few of us have the true gift, Mr Cookson."

"Right." He pats the bar and glances at the clock. It's dead on twelve. He moves to the door and swings it open, wedging it in place. "Well, is that everything?"

"I'm sorry?"

"Is there anything else I can help you with? On the phone, you said you wanted to talk. Was that all? It's opening time and I really should... get on."

She fixes him with an earnest stare. "I'd like to hold a psychic evening here, Mr Cookson. Here, in your pub." She smiles, an unexpected beam, allowing her conceit to abate for a moment.

"A what?"

"I want to talk to the spirits. The town is awash with them, in such an unusual concentration. This building in particular has so much history. It's the oldest pub in town, I believe?"

Chris nods briefly—it's all he's allowed before she continues.

"Then, this is the ideal place. Indeed, it's the *only* place."

Rona walks the long way to work, idling along the streets and the side roads to avoid people. She has enough of people at work. Beforehand, she likes the silence. And there's always silence in this town; moments when traffic ceases and birds forget to sing.

She barely has time to scan the bar and note how many people are already in when she hears, "Hey, Ro."

"Hi, Sam. The usual?" Rona turns and smiles widely.

"Yeah, and keep them coming."

Rona glances at her watch. "It's only half five. Bad day?"

"Girlfriend stuff. Again." He shakes his head and makes a few grumbling sounds.

"Oh. I'm sorry."

"She's on about us getting married, having kids, and shit like that. *When will you ask me, Sam? When do I get a ring, Sam? Blah-blah's doing it.* I'm only twenty-four. What do I want that kind of shit for?"

"Have you talked to her? Properly, I mean. Asked her why it's so important." Rona sets the pint glass on the bar, and Sam sifts through the coins from his pocket.

"Yeah. She said if I loved her, I'd marry her." He snorts into his glass. "Well, it's bollocks. Of course I love her. But, marriage? It's so... so..."

"Final?"

He shrugs. "Ah. I don't get her. She's the same age as me. She's home now, baking or sewing, or whatever it is she does. Feels like I'm living with my mother half the time." He stops abruptly and smiles with tight lips. "Never tell her I said that!"

Awkwardly, as though unsure how to extricate himself from the conversation, he takes his glass and moves across to the dartboard.

The pub slowly fills—some people taking a detour on their way home from work, others already out for the evening. The sun dips behind the hill, candles are lit, the air becomes thick with stale-sweet sweat.

Outside, for a breather, Rona's eyes sweep across the river. For a moment, I'm standing alongside her. For a brief moment, I am myself, with heartache for my own lost love flooding through me. I am filling up with affection and sadness and the aching emptiness of grief, for the first time in so many years.

Rona shudders. She knows I'm here, barely concealing her alarm from the people passing her to enter the pub. One or two pause to ask if she's okay, and she smiles weakly and nods, not trusting herself.

And then I am lost in the collective again, and those emotions fade before I can seize them. She laughs at herself for such imaginings, convincing herself these things cannot possibly be real. *We* know, however, things beyond our control are happening here.

The air around Rona is not still. As she walks home, as she passes the late-night burger bar and drops in for a cheeseburger and chips, as she dawdles along the road not especially wanting to go home, the air is not still.

We know she can feel us. We don't mean to scare her. In truth, we are lost, wandering as aimlessly as she is, remnants of ourselves. With Rona, we've found a connection we thought gone forever.

At the front door of her building, she stares up at her window, hesitating. She feels for the keys in her pocket and squeezes them into her palm. Her ground-floor neighbour is playing music; she nods her head along with the beat as she passes, but it's only a murmur once she's in her own flat. Knowing someone is close enough to come running should she scream is a comfort. It's only been a few months since Murray was killed a short distance from here. She's unaware he's still pacing back and forth, refusing to accept the truth.

Rona nibbles at the cheeseburger as she wanders to the fridge for a cider, kicks her shoes into the corner, drops onto the sofa, and switches on the television. She yawns and feels the heaviness of her head.

Not for the first time, she wonders if she should go home, back to her mother who'll be furious and relieved and tender and domineering in equal measure—planning Rona's return to university or pushing her into the first dead-end job she can conjure.

Ah... Rona nods to herself and takes another bite, *that's* why she shouldn't.

As the road outside empties and people tuck themselves up for the night, Rona has a quick shower before bed.

Helen. Where's Helen? Is she here?

Rona opens her eyes, frozen beneath her covers, eyes shifting left and right in the darkness. I feel her fear. I feel the ferryman's anguish. More than I should. Emotions are for the living; we have no use for them. We do not *feel* because we cannot influence. The ferryman treads his own path; he clings to his grief and will not relinquish it.

"Who's Helen?" Rona asks, summoning enough voice to be heard. She looks straight at me. "Why are you looking for her?"

It's been so long since I attempted to speak. I wasn't here a moment ago; I wasn't the one who called for Helen. I was drifting, observing, carrying out my obligations.

It wasn't me, I try to explain, but I'm already fading.

***

"So, what do you make of all this psychic business?" Chris is pinning Jane Markham's posters onto the wooden beams beside the bar, tutting to himself.

"Dunno. It might be fun. Might bring some new customers in. We'll wow them with our craft ale."

"Should never have agreed. It's all nonsense."

"You've got to admit there's something stifling about this town. Can't you feel it? The air, it's so... heavy."

"Nope, never felt that. It's just the same as any other place."

"You've always lived here, though, right? Perhaps you're immune."

Chris finishes taping the posters to the walls while Rona stares at the glasses on the bar. She should be putting them away, but she's motionless, lost in thoughts that have no shape.

"Don't tell me you believe in ghosts."

"Maybe I've seen one." She glances at the corner, at the table where the candle wouldn't light.

It's happened more than once, and she always sees the same face. Her response isn't as dramatic as the first time. When the candle doesn't light, she prepares herself. Sometimes she keeps her eye on him; sometimes she walks away and ignores him.

She thinks about the horse that reared up and almost trampled her.

She pictures the lone boat that rows up and down the river without a sound.

"I've owned this place for almost fifteen years, and I've never had a problem with *things that go bump in the night*."

"Maybe you haven't been looking." Her voice is more playful than she feels.

"This Jane Markham woman says we're swamped with them." He laughs. "Perhaps I ought to make a plaque."

***

We watch over the town with languid indifference. We watch as if a play or a film were unfolding in front of us. For the most recent souls to have passed, the play is more relevant, because the actors are their children, their husbands and wives, their friends. They stalk the living, desperate for one last interaction. They sense their attachment waning; they fight against it.

The rest of us have existed in this manner much longer than we lived in our mortal bodies. For us, the world has changed, the people have changed, and we no longer relate to any form of it. We watch these people living out their months and years, so tied to the minutiae of each day, so pinned down by duty and expectation, so unaware how quickly it will be over. Yet we are remote, objective.

And, because of this, our reactions to Rona—our concern, our enchantment—have surprised and confounded us. We tread cautiously beside her.

Rona does not sleep easily. The memory of her dreams, of the ghosts residing within them, prevents her from settling. Because they must be dreams, mustn't they? Her eyes become heavy, despite herself; and her body slackens. She floats or swims or glides through the air—immersed in the tranquillity of a smooth river, with the contentment of everything being well.

She cries out, ripped from her sleep, dripping with sweat and shivering uncontrollably. Her eyes are wide, seeking something from the dark corners of the room. But what? In the dream, she knew exactly what she was looking for, but now she has no idea, save for a few vague images that surface.

There's movement in the room. Nothing she can pinpoint, but the air is not still.

She makes a hot drink and perches on the edge of the sofa, hands wrapped around it as though it's the coldest day of winter. Soon, the sun will rise and flood the room with light, and she'll be drawn into a new day. She focuses on that thought, waiting for the first birds to sing for the dawn,

*

"Mummy?" She immediately regrets the word. It was the first thing that came into her head. When did she last call her mother Mummy, anyway?

"Rona? What's wrong?"

"I need to ask you a question, about when I was little."

"How are you? I've been worried."

"You needn't be. I'm fine."

"How do I know you're not just saying that to get me off your back? I have to worry about you because you won't tell me anything."

Rona bites her tongue because she needs to ask her question and doesn't want to be diverted by argument and accusation.

"There's nothing to tell. Honestly. I'm thinking things through." Her mother is keen on thinking and planning. Thinking is a good reason to be alone.

In truth, the more she ponders it, her reason for being in this particular town eludes her. It's almost as though she were guided here.

"Do you need money? Are you in trouble? Are you hiding from the police?"

Rona bursts into laughter. "Hiding from the police? Really?"

After a moment, her mother joins in. "Okay, I admit it was a long shot. I'm sorry. I'll try to... You said you had a question."

Rona takes a breath, uncertain how to proceed. It had seemed so important when she was dialling. "When I was little, when we lived in Glanville Row, you told me I sleep-walked. You said I turned on the lights when you were asleep and moved the furniture around. Is that right?"

"Yes." A long, drawn-out sound; a hint of trepidation "Two or three times a month, I'd come down in the morning and the sofa would be on the other side of the room, or the telly would be upside down, or the table would be pushed against the patio doors. The lights would be on all around the house. And you'd be asleep in the corner, looking so angelic."

110

"Mum," Rona says softly, gently. "I was three when we left that house. I couldn't *reach* the light switches. I certainly wouldn't have been able to move the table by myself."

Her mother is silent. There are rustling sounds, and sighs, as her mother tries to figure out what to say next.

"Mum... was our house haunted? Did I see ghosts?" Her words are careful and precise. And she waits, anticipating nothing. She's prepared—hoping, even—for a swift denial and a hasty retreat.

Rona imagines her mother hunching forward as if to whisper in her ear.

"I don't know. Why? Have you remembered something?"

"I'm not sure."

"Are you scared? Were you scared back then?"

"No," she answers quickly, assuaging her mother's imminent guilt. "No, nothing like that. I think I'm seeing ghosts here too."

"Oh, Rona. Please come home."

She wishes she could retract her last sentence. "I live in an old building. And I work in an old pub. I'm probably imagining it all. Don't worry. I'm fine. Everything's fine. I promise." This is where they started. "I have to go. Love you."

"Rona, don't—"

We knew she was special, our beautiful child. We knew there was a reason we were drawn to her above anyone else.

***

Around town, people argue whether ghosts are real, if psychics can really channel the spirits. The debate is provoked by the posters advertising Jane Markham's show tonight. Jane Markham herself sits outside a café on the high street, enjoying the soothing ease of the town, enjoying her cappuccino and a slice of pear and ginger cake. She's unaware, it seems, that beside her, several souls are converging.

How can that be? we ask ourselves, allowing ourselves to be concerned.

Every so often, she writes in the notebook open on the table, her writing so small and neat she fits two lines of text for every printed line on the paper. She smooths the pages when she's finished, leans back, takes another sip of coffee, and waits for the next thought to form. We wonder what she's writing; we would so much like poetry to be emanating from her, beautiful lines of verse that prove she's not as controlled and pinched as she appears. But we suspect we are wrong.

A hum of excitement flows around the Boatman. Jane Markham waits behind the door marked PRIVATE, and at precisely eight o'clock, she makes her entrance, no longer in her tailored trouser suit but wearing a long floral dress that floats as she walks. She bows her head and crosses her arms against her chest with insincere humility. I'm reminded of the way Catholic nuns would walk in silent pairs. She raises her head and smiles benevolently at the twenty or so people waiting for her.

"Welcome. I have spoken with the spirit world my entire life. As a child, it terrified me. But as I grew up, I realised it was a gift from the universe which I needed to share, to allow people, *you*" —she opens her arms to encircle the room—"to hear from loved ones who have passed." She looks towards the ceiling and raises her arms higher. "To the spirits in this room, step forward and be known."

The audience is silent, bated. Most have their eyes fixed on Jane herself, while others glance uneasily at the darkest corners of the room, at the shadows.

Jane closes her eyes and nods. "I have a tall gentleman here. Wery proud, very proper. Medals on his chest. I see a date. 1944. Is it Albert?" The room is silent. "No, not Albert. Charles?" She shakes her head, appears to be listening intently. "It's okay. You can step forward. Tell me who you are. William? W... Walter?"

"Wilfred?" says a voice from the middle table. An elderly lady is holding a younger woman's hand—her daughter.

"Wilfred! Yes!" Jane holds out a hand to the voice. "He was a good, kind man, wasn't he? He's showing me a baby on his knee. He was..." She tilts her head. "Your father?"

"My uncle."

"Ah, yes, he's telling me that now. Can I just say, he loved you like a daughter." She pauses again. "His medals were very important to him. He keeps showing them to me. Was it... army?"

"Yes." There's sadness in the poor woman's voice.

"And he died before the end of the war? 1944?"

"Yes. He was twenty-nine. I don't remember him. I was a baby."

"He says he watched over you, watched you grow up. He's very proud of you and your family. He wants you to know that. Do you know where the medals are?"

"I have them."

"He's saying..." Jane's face breaks into a smile, refined and rehearsed. "He's saying he'd like you to polish them more often. They never get polished, he's saying."

Amid a ripple of laughter, she turns to the room and begins again.

The ferryman follows Rona as she collects glasses. She senses his touch on her shoulder, but only fleetingly; a bristle, a chill, hardly anything. We see her turn her head or pause as if listening to something indistinct.

Many souls are lined patiently, one behind the other, snaking around the room, between the tables and the living. An Elizabethan gentleman; a farmer of indistinguishable era; a scullery maid in from my own time. An elderly lady with too many shawls is expectant but bewildered. A young mother and her infant boy are charred with soot. Soldiers, so many ill-fated men from all wars, all centuries—some are as bright and willing as they were on their first deployment, others are battle-weary and bloodied, hoarding memories no one should have to carry.

Jane Markham doesn't see them. Indeed, she can't see them. Our fears are realised. She's a charlatan. She lies. She makes up people who are not here. She tells people their loved ones are well, happy, no longer in pain. When difficult questions are asked, she shakes her head with regret and says the spirit has faded.

Rona, when we seek her out in the dusky light, is full of fright. Her eyes are wide, her lips slightly parted as if a scream is already surfacing. She stares at the line of souls, holding her breath and trying to be as still as possible.

For reasons we have no control over, we have been made apparent to her. Her eyes are pulled into a frown, flickering across each ghostly face as it sharpens and clarifies. Her fingers tighten around the glass she's holding; she gropes her way back behind the bar for some sort of protection. Her hands shake. Her head throbs with the spectral vibrations, with the impression of voices rising.

But all they're doing is waiting, hoping for their turn. And slowly Rona begins to see them for what they are. Ghosts, spirits —isolated creatures yearning for contact with the outside world. One smiles coyly, uncertain of the rules or the response she'll receive, and Rona—our amazing, intuitive child—smiles back.

Jane Markham is talking about a woman called Vera, although there is no soul close to her. Rona watches the performance, a dramatic tale of jealousy and secret wills unfolding—and the rapt audience member who's nodding and agreeing with everything— and realises Jane is oblivious to the ghosts in front of her.

Rona steps from behind the bar and reaches out her hand to the spirit nearest to her, tentatively, with child-like wonder. The soul, a soldier from the Great War, is overwhelmed that, after all this time dead, this girl can see him, can examine the wounds he carries and the scars he bears. In the middle of this busy room, time stands still. Two people converge across the centuries, both equally spellbound.

Perhaps Rona expected to feel something physical—an opaque chill, something solid beneath her fingers. Instead, intense emotion engulfs her—loneliness, pain, regret, sorrow.

She gasps as she pulls away, and several people glance across. She feels the same hollowness I felt when I was cast from her dream. She wraps her arms around her torso, the iciness and up-heaval lingering.

"Can she not see them?" she mutters under her breath so only we can hear. "Can she not hear them?"

Jane closes her eyes and holds her hands open in front of her. Centring herself to receive the next spirit. She draws her hands towards her chest. "Okay," she says softly. "I have a young man with a motorcycle..."

Rona shakes her head. She can't see a motorbike; she can see the Victorian scullery maid who is next in line.

The poor souls are becoming restless, shifting around, drifting away. Those who remain are stubbornly determined or oblivious Jane Markham is a fraud. All they want is for their story to be told, their peace to be sought.

Rona moves slowly around the room, pretending to clear the tables. She whispers to the nearest soul, "What's your name?"

There's a growing confidence in her, a purpose; our beautiful child is now our voice. We watch as she's folded into the story of this soul, by all the stories they have to offer. Rona absorbs the information; we see her filling up, a light shining from her. She smiles, endearingly, honoured to be trusted with the entirety of another life.

She moves on, connecting with another, then another. She begins her journey with enthusiasm and sincerity, but as the minutes pass—as the centuries are shared with her, many times over—she becomes distressed, burdened, close to tears.

"Too much," she whispers to no one. "Too much pain and sadness."

It's a small pub with low ceilings and dark wooden beams. It's oppressive with so many people crammed inside. Rona stumbles as she tries to escape and is suddenly face-to-face with Jane. Her eyes narrow on poor Rona; she turns away, scathingly. Rona slinks back against the wall, feeling the smooth, cool stone beneath her fingers. She remains close. She cannot pull herself away.

"I can feel a young woman beside me. She's holding a bouquet of flowers, roses and daisies. She has such an open face, but she's tinged with sadness. Elizabeth?... Jane?... Mary?" A woman at the front glances up. "Oh, she's so softly spoken. Martha?"

The woman at the front nods. "My aunt was Martha."

Jane furrows her brows. "Yes, my dear. She's nodding at me. She was young when she passed? I ask because she's in her wedding dress."

"Forty-five."

"She loved her wedding day. She's showing off her dress to me because it's special to her. She tries to be close by whenever she can. She brings the scent of flowers with her. Do you unexpectedly smell flowers around you?"

"I suppose I do, yes."

"That's her, letting you know she's with you all."

"Oh, thank you. Um, my mother—her sister—passed about six months ago. I was hoping she might be here?"

Jane's eyes narrow, her lips purse. Rona steps forward. We hold our breath.

"Yes, she is," Rona says, loud enough for people to turn to face her. "Ivy's right here. She was so pleased you wore purple to her funeral." An elderly woman holds Rona's hand, her eyes twinkling with delight. She shares her story without words, and behind her, a tall handsome man appears.

"Is she with Martha?"

Rona bows and glances at Jane with contempt. "I'm afraid Martha *isn't* here. Ivy's with your father. I see them both. He's so happy they've been reunited—he disliked being apart from her, even in life, didn't he? Never knew what to do with himself."

The woman nods with tears forming in her eyes. "No, he didn't. Silly old sod would sit at the window like a puppy waiting for her."

"He keeps playing with the curls in her hair, twirling them with his fingers." Ivy smiles and Rona sees the young woman Ivy once was. "She had such wonderfully golden hair. He called her his goddess."

"Oh, he did, all the time."

"Excuse me," Jane interjects from her spot on the stage. "Do you mind? This is my show."

"But you're not…" Rona trails off. *You're not doing it right*, she was going to say. But the way Jane, Chris, and the audience are all staring, she falters. The room is silent, and after a moment's uncertainty, she flees to the kitchen.

"What was all that about?" Chris appears in the doorway—a small arch with saloon-style doors.

"Sorry, I just got caught up."

"People have paid to see the show, not you have some kind of breakdown."

"It wasn't—"

"You planned it, didn't you, with that woman in the audience? It was staged to take the piss? You can't really see…" He shakes his head and laughs at how ridiculous his question was going to be. He points at her. "You almost had me."

In truth, she doesn't know what's happening, doesn't fully understand. And we don't know how to explain. Back in the bar, she vows merely to observe, but her displeasure deepens and her exasperation rises.

"Can't she see them?" she asks again, feeling all the despair we feel. Chris shoots her a warning glare. "What? She's a fraud. She hasn't got a single thing right. They're feeding her the answers, and they don't even realise it. Everything she says is so vague they all think she's talking to them."

Instead of the sixty-year-old woman Jane claims she's speaking with, a young boy stands beside her. He's wheezing and hunched over, blinking as though the lights are hurting his eyes. His face is smeared with soot.

"That's how it works. It's entertainment. It's not real. No one thinks it's real."

Rona merely smiles and turns away. Oh, how differently she knows.

She tries not to listen anymore. She tries to focus on the drinks she's serving and ignore the room. But it's difficult. There's too much going on around her, too many voices. She sees every-thing—unexpected, unwarranted, unwelcome even. The truth is right here: the dead remain with you, they watch over you, they observe and protect you. We can be heard, and we can hear you. But not everyone is honoured with this gift—and you can't decide whether it's you, or Jane Markham, or our beautiful Rona who hears. We choose.

"Two pints, Ro," Sam says, appearing at the bar and pushing the correct money towards her. "Quite a crowd she's brought in."

"Yeah. Didn't think we'd see you tonight. I didn't think this would be your kind of thing."

He nods to a table in the corner. "The other half wanted to come. Do you think she'll predict me some lottery numbers?"

"You never know, Sam."

"You all right? You're not your usual self."

"I'm fine. I don't like this woman very much, that's all. She's a total fake."

"Aren't they all?"

Rona reflects for a moment. "If you'd asked me yesterday, I'd have agreed with you."

"And now?"

She glances over at the stage and clicks her tongue. "Now, I know better." She shakes her head. "No, no, no," she mutters. "No."

This final *no* is a shout. Sam and several others turn to her; some scowl, a few laugh.

"Can't you see him? He's right there in front of you. He's called Joseph, and he was the ferryman who took people across the river before the bridge was built. He wants you to listen to him."

First, people look at Rona, astounded by the sincerity in her voice; then at Jane Markham who's floundering, battling to stay calm and serene in front of witnesses, while anger flows through her.

"He's looking for Helen," Rona continues.

A hand in the audience rises hesitantly. "I'm Helen."

"I'm sorry," Rona says. "The Helen he's looking for is no longer living. She's a spirit. She's out there somewhere, but he can't find her."

Joseph gazes in wonder at Rona. "I loved her so very much," he says.

"I know."

"She was to be my bride. Have you seen her?"

"No, I haven't. Perhaps she's here?"

Joseph casts his gaze around the room and shakes his head despondently. "No. She is lost." He sounds so sad; and we realise we're all sad, just a little.

Joseph bows his head, his grief and anguish overwhelming him. We despair. We feel everything he is feeling. We do not understand why Helen is not already a part of us, either. At some point, she has become separated, alone in her watery grave. We see no happy ending.

We feel more than we should. The strength of Joseph's attachment to his beloved Helen contaminates us. With Rona so close, it's intensifying.

Joseph holds Rona's hand; she feels the pressure of it. "Thank you for hearing me." And he almost smiles—almost smiles for the first time in over a century.

I want my turn. I want my story to be heard. I want Rona to listen to me, with all the compassion she can offer. But I'm pulled away with the collective. Dragged away. If I still had corporeal hands, they would be clawing at the furniture, trying to break free.

The bar is silent and shadowy after Jane Markham storms away with great theatre and intense vocabulary, and the dazed audience dwindles. Rona sits alone, her feet on the chair and knees pulled tight into her torso.

"All right?" Chris asks.

She shakes her head.

"Here." He pushes a glass towards her. "Brandy."

"I don't like it."

"It'll calm you down."

"I don't understand what happened. I saw them. Ghosts. So many of them."

Chris says nothing. He sits opposite her and swigs his own drink. He doesn't understand, so he cannot comfort her. Instead, he holds her hand as it rests on the table.

"I know how stupid it sounds. I've made a fool of myself." She glances towards the door. "They'll be talking about this for years. I should be going."

"You can stay here if you don't want to be alone. We've got a free room in the B&B tonight."

"No, I'll be fine." She stands and downs the brandy in one gulp with a grimace. "Nope, I still don't like that stuff. Thanks for not sacking me tonight."

"At least let me walk you home," he says, feeling helpless.

"No, honestly, I'll be fine. I need to clear my head."

Joseph walks with Rona, and Rona finds reassurance in turn. With our voices eager to be heard, his presence calms her. We sense his intentions, as clear as if they were ours, and we fear for our beautiful child.

They walk through the streets because Rona—despite what she told Chris—doesn't yet want to return to her small flat, with its eerie shadows and unexplained noises. She's safer in the open, with the living in easy reach. She peers around each corner, down every narrow alleyway; she stares at the faces of people walking towards her. In everyone and everything, she looks for signs of the next life.

Rona crosses her arms against her body and shivers uncontrollably. A wind blows around her which doesn't seem to disturb anyone else. The whispers of the dead ripple like waves on the river.

Finally, she runs out of roads to walk and stands outside her building. She imagines all the souls who may be living alongside her, breathing air from decades, centuries ago. And I know the time, *my* turn, is approaching. Joseph withdraws, sliding back towards his boat on the river, resuming his customary search.

Helen, he whispers, and Rona is uneasy.

You understand.

"Who's there?" Her voice is surprisingly soft and sympathetic, albeit with an edge of apprehension.

I am. But I am not formed; I am not myself. I have no shape. It's been too long since my death to fully recreate my physical self. I am a whisper, a sensation, a vague outline.

It's late. The town is small enough to fall asleep after dark. Indeed, it's quieter than during my lifetime when fishermen and traders rose before dawn. Rona is drowsy on her sofa, nestling a glass of wine in her hand, half-watching a film.

Or she was, a moment ago.

"Who's there?" she repeats.

I'm here. I'm… I'm… Who am I? I knew yesterday, I'm sure I did. I knew my name when the Luftwaffe flew high in the skies above us; I knew when Gladstone and Disraeli battled in Parliament, one ascending over the other. I knew when Napoleon was defeated and at the death and succession of many monarchs. Matthew? It sounds familiar. I think I am Matthew.

"Matthew?" she says. "What do you want? Why are you here?"

"Don't be scared." My voice startles me, a penetrating Devonshire lilt.

"I don't think I'm scared, Matthew. Why are you here?"

"Because I lived in this building a long time ago," I say, becoming conscious of the fact only as I speak the words. "I lived in these rooms when the road outside was cobbled and there were buildings all around, packed on top of each other."

I know these rooms have changed, but I cannot pinpoint how or when. I see all the years, all at once. The memories of my life are a blur, as though I've been spinning on the spot, the way of a small child, and I'm only just finding focus again.

121

"When you looked out of the window," I continue, the details becoming a stream, "you could see new buildings being erected everywhere. It was a wonderful, prosperous time. So many people coming into town, so many opportunities. This house was *my* new beginning."

Sadness overwhelms me as the stream becomes a flood. A whole lifetime poured over me in a few seconds. Oh, the heartbreak and joy. It's too much—too much for Rona when she was in the pub, too much for me now.

"Did you... die here?"

I close my eyes. "Yes."

She shudders and looks around her, wondering in which corner I met my end, which of the floorboards bear the stains of my passing. She wonders if it was a peaceful end or borne of violence. As the memories become more vivid, I can answer her; I am scarred with the pain of my passing. And it *was* painful. It was violent. I was murdered.

I carry so many dark secrets I wonder how I lived so long, how I avoided others who had been treated so badly by me. I was a thief, a scoundrel, a pirate. But I lived to repent my sins. I turned a page. I fell in love.

"My betrothed did not know of my past. I was new in town. I had money—procured by dishonest means, but money, nonetheless. I had the illusion of power and grandeur, and that, it seems, was all that mattered. I took this house and employed servants."

I laugh. It's absurd to think, after my humble beginnings and my outlaw ways, I settled as a gentleman.

Outside the window, I see the cobbled street, the imposing yet identical houses on the opposite side of the road. I see carriages and horses, and ladies in their finery parading on a Sunday after church, arm-in-arm with friends or husbands. I see the sunshine of a summer's day.

"In Plymouth, before I came here, I lived in squalor. I had nothing but the clothes on my back. I stole what I needed. I drank and gambled. I owed a lot of money to a lot of people."

Rona sits on the edge of the sofa, her arms crossed over her knees, her shoulders hunched, listening intently.

"One day, a large ship arrived from the West Indies. Over the course of the following days, I managed to steal from that ship everything I needed and more, so much more. In those few days, I became rich, and no one suspected. I should have repaid my debts, of course—which would have been the sensible thing to do. But I was young and greedy, and I am ashamed to admit it, I fled in the middle of the night.

"I found myself here, taking lodgings, at first, then as I settled, this house. And I fell in love with the most wonderful woman." I fall silent at the thought of my perfect Catherine, and here she is before me, her smile illuminating the room and her dark hair tumbling around her shoulders. She's wearing her favourite red dress, the dress she married in. But she isn't really here. We have not been reunited because my soul is not worthy of her.

"That's so sad," Rona says, nudging me out of my reverie.

"Perhaps. But she saved me. Everything I had been and done before was forgotten. She changed me into a decent and honest man, in part. I was still hiding, of course, still avoiding my debts. Although, by then, the debt would have been impossible to pay. To abscond in such a manner, from such terrible people, meant my forfeit would have been my life.

"We lived a good, happy life for three years. Three wonderful years with my wife, and I thought I was safe. But my creditor would not have it that way. I was found, or I was given up by someone I thought a friend. As I suspected, he no longer had interest in the money, and I was struck down.

"My Catherine, who was thankfully in Bristol recovering from illness when I was attacked, found my body when she returned a fortnight later. I watched as she entered the room, covering her mouth from the stench, and upon discovering me, collapsed into the most anguished cry I have ever heard. How much I wanted to save her from that moment. I tried to reach out to her, but the world dissolved beneath my fingers."

Outside, the cobbles have disappeared. It's the street as it is now I see again. Cars are parked along the road. Trees not even planted then tower above the roofs.

"I lost Catherine. When I fully understood how the spirit world functioned, I searched for her, but she was gone. Maybe she remarried and our connection was dissolved; maybe she died too soon afterwards. She had not been well for a long time—the shock of it may well have seen her off. But I don't know for certain."

I am icy when I reach the end of my tale. I *feel* the cold. I wanted to tell my story, to have it heard in its entirety, because in the end, that's all we have to give. But I wish I hadn't. I wish I hadn't seen my Catherine again, because I am bereft once more, the pain as sharp now as it was then. I retreat; I cannot stay in this room a moment longer. Around me, your world evaporates, and I am absorbed and welcomed back.

There's a reason we become one. It saves us from the torture of remembering who we once were—for good or for bad—and what we had to give up. It's a comfort to observe our lives, our stories, without grief. There's a reason why this is best.

***

The air is not still. The breeze washes around Rona, fresh after the claustrophobic heat of the past few days. Listening carefully, she hears a whispered voice instructing her, guiding her. Not our voice; not mine. Her face is pale, her eyes are blank and distant, the way a sleepwalker stares into their dream rather than into the real world. She stands at the bank of the river, her body stiff and unyielding. The ferryman rips through the water towards her.

Joseph alights from his boat and offers his hand. "Helen, my love, finally."

"I'm not Helen." But her words are lost, her conviction uncertain.

Reality drips away. She reaches to accept his hand, warm and corporeal. How is it possible? We are equally in awe and alarmed at the potential. Joseph helps her step over the low wall dividing the path from the shingle. It crunches beneath her, stabbing sharp edges into her bare feet. He holds her gaze, walking backwards into the water, with an encouraging, tender smile. One step at a time, the way a parent would persuade a scared child.

"Helen," he says again, and the more he repeats the name, the more she believes it.

Rona, for she is still Rona though only just, is knee-deep in the water, and we can do nothing but watch—we don't have the capacity. Her hair becomes longer and darker, unkempt. Her jeans and T-shirt become a long, full-skirted dress with a tight bodice and lace trim. Our perception is being manipulated so we see what Joseph sees. The power of desperate love is unfathomable.

Our voices are unheard. We try to call out; we are repressed. Rona wades further until she's thigh-high, then waist-high. We pray the chill of the water will revive her. Her lips are moving as though she's muttering something, either to Joseph or to herself, but no matter how hard we strain, we cannot hear her.

Chest-high now. Water laps across her shoulders, her hair drifts on the surface Helen's treasured topaz pendant floats on the current. She walks further. Her feet leave the bottom, the water too deep. Joseph cradles her until she's lying flat, floating.

Her garments become heavy, the garments that are not real but a figment of our collective imagination. And this heaviness begins to pull her under.

We strive to reach her, our beautiful child, but she is beyond us, between worlds. A smile glistens on her lips; the water slowly consumes her.

Joseph strokes her brow, lowering his mouth to her ear and whispering—words full of promises he can't keep. He kisses her cheek and holds her steady under the water. Another victim this river, this town, has claimed. We hold hands and keep vigil. How long has it been? How soon before she awakens into her next life?

Time has no meaning for us. A second, an hour: all the same. We bow our heads and pray. We can only wait.

"Rona! Rona!"

Splash!

Gasp!

Scream!

Alarm and commotion. Movement of every kind shatters the fantasy.

Panicking, surging forward to the river. Chris dives in and pulls Rona to the surface. He came from nowhere, this saviour, our hero, dragging her from the water and onto the beach.

Lying on the shingle, Rona violently coughs up river water, painfully grasping for oxygen. She was at home. How is she here? She was in bed. She had a dream. It was just a dream.

She sits suddenly, and Chris tries to hold her. She remembers. She searches the darkness frantically.

"It was him—the ferryman. Can you see him? Is he still here?" Her breathing is laboured as she drags the night air into her lungs.

"There's no one here," Chris says, smoothing her hair, recovering slowly from his own shock. "You slipped. You fell."

"No. He took me. The ferryman. He brought me here. I wanted to go with him."

"Go where, Rona? There's no one here."

He folds his arms around her, and she collapses into his embrace. She sobs agonisingly, the sound of it echoing around the houses and walls, across the river and back. Chris doesn't let go. He wraps his jacket around her and protects her from the fear he cannot see.

We withdraw, assured she'll be safe from further harm. We withdraw into our anguish.

It was our fault. We interfered for our own gratification and unintentionally amplified Joseph's need to find Helen. We came too close to the living world when she should have been observing from afar, to satisfy our curiosity, nothing more. We should have been drifting away, not drawing closer.

So, we pull away, soaring above the town which was once our home. With sadness and regret—tangible feelings which have been lost to us for so long. Our beautiful child, so fragile yet so vibrant, realises how close to death she came, realises how easy it can be.

ACKNOWLEDGEMENTS

This collection is a reissue of a book released in 2014 by Vagabondage Press, originally published as Our Beautiful Child.

However, this is more than a reissue, it's a revision, with some changes to the characters, their names, and in some cases their motivations.

For people who have read this collection previously, the Boathouse pub is the Boatman in this version—named after the pub which inspired the stories, and which has itself been renamed since 2014 and the building repurposed as a restaurant. In renaming it, I hope to keep it alive for everyone who remembers it.

Therefore, to avoid confusion, the boatman character in the original stories is now the ferryman.

Thank you to Karen Sanders Editing for casting her eye over my comma addiction. And to Wendy, Tina, Jennifer, and Christine who voted for the winning title. Congratulations to Luisa who entered a draw via my newsletter and won a character named after her. A special shout-out to Jennifer Martain who helped greatly with inspiration for the cover art.

***

If you enjoyed this book, please consider leaving a review on the retailer's website, and any other site you may use. Please tell your friends about it. Thank you.

ABOUT THE AUTHOR

Annalisa Crawford lives in Cornwall, UK, with a good supply of moorland and beaches to keep her inspired. She lives with her husband, and canine writing partner, Artoo. Her two sons have flown the nest, but still like a mention.

Annalisa writes dark contemporary, character-driven stories, with a hint of paranormal.

She is the author of four short story collections, and her novels Grace & Serenity (July 2020) and Small Forgotten Moments (August 2021) are published by Vine Leaves Press.

For more information visit
www.annalisacrawford.com

Printed in Great Britain
by Amazon

39306656R00078